PRAISE FOR *ASYLUM*

"Relentlessly researched, *Asylum* is a burning poem of a novel. Its existence is payback for paternalism and the narcissistic dark side of early Western medicine."
　　　—Stacey Levine, author of *The Girl with Brown Fur*

"Lush and vertiginous, *Asylum* offers a pointed analysis of obsession and power early in the development of psychiatry. A fierce look at how some bodies strive to control other bodies by submitting them to the tyranny of the gaze, of the camera, of touch, always in the name of health. And yet, how easy it is for the tables to be turned, for the observed to imperceptibly slip into the role of observer..."
　　　—Brian Evenson, author of *The Glassy, Burning Floor of Hell*

"Bold, dynamic, gorgeously written ... a wonderful catawampus-ing of the love story; and a richly researched investigation into power, desire, and narrative possibility."
　　　—Lance Olsen, author of *Skin Elegies*

"A gorgeously imagined glimpse into the relationship of Charcot to his famous patient, Augustine. ... A delicious novel that flays its characters to their dark, deeply human hearts."
　　　—Tina May Hall, author of *The Snow Collectors*

"In *Asylum*, Shope fulfills the promise of her debut, *Hangings*, with another work that sears the literary firmament. This is a dan~~c~~
text, cutting edge text, as bold as Augus~~tine~~ ~~
ney into the human condition with ~~a~~
lessly transformative combat of cod~~e~~

pretense as they struggle for psychic survival crippled with vulner-abilities both terrible and redemptive. Shope achieves tour de force narrative that at its darkest deepest density still manages to dance across the page, every sentence, every paragraph leaving the reader adrift in wonder world before venturing on to the next note. *Asylum* solidifies Nina Shope's place as one of the strongest, strangest, most provocative writers there's ever been. *Asylum* got so much heart it's a wonder the book don't explode in your hand instead of waiting till it has buried itself soul deep, sanctifying everything it touches with that lingering sense of imaginative wonder that only literature of a certain stature and significance can provide. This work is not an asylum, this work is a sanctuary."

—Arthur R. Flowers, author of *Another Good Loving Blues*
and *The Hoodoo Book of Flowers*

"*Asylum* is historical fiction at its most intimate as we peer deeply into the interior of Augustine, a patient being treated for hysteria by nineteenth-century charismatic neurologist Charcot. The hospital is theatre, and the theatre involves both doctor and patient in a danger-ous interplay of seduction and power. We feel the claustrophobia of obsession within each finely wrought sentence, and as we long for Augustine's escape, we are pressed at each turn to interrogate the very nature of escape and the possibilities of freedom experienced within the self."

—Jessie van Eerden, author of *Call It Horses*

ASYLUM

ASYLUM

— A NOVEL —

NINA SHOPE

DZANC
BOOKS

2580 Craig Rd.
Ann Arbor, MI 48103
www.dzancbooks.org

Library of Congress Cataloging-in-Publication Data Available Upon Request

ISBN: 978-1950539512
First US edition: May 2022
Interior design by Michelle Dotter
Cover by Matthew Revert

Thank you to the following publications for printing early excerpts from the novel:
Plinth. "Asylum."
Starcher-Blog. "The Clinic."
Sidebrow. "Three Fragments."
Fourteen Hills: The SFSU Review. "The Clinic."

Printed in the United States of America

10 9 8 7 6 5 4 3 2 1

for Augustine

Hystéro-Épilepsie Contracture, Augustine, Paris, 1878

I.

The Clinic
1875

You stand at the front of the amphitheatre, chalk in hand, the right side of your face drooping like a stroke victim's. Your hand curving inward, clenched, right leg dragging behind your left so it resembles a vestigial appendage, a half-amputated limb.

You play to the crowd, ape paralysis, distort your countenance until they almost cease to recognize you, wondering if you have not in fact escaped the wards, if you are actually an inmate imitating the great professor. Charcot, *le Maître*. Cold. Aloof. With a face like an undertaker's. Under your black stovepipe hat. Your dark coat that always smells of damp wool.

Your entire body is dedicated to this performance of paralysis, the illusion only ruptured when you add to the illustrations on the blackboard—standing straight to draw more accurately, coloring the muscles along the right side of a chalked skull a bright and glaring red, as though you have peeled back the board to expose flesh. Only then do you relax the muscles of your mouth, your arm, your leg. Only then do you return to yourself. The audience applauding your transformation.

Tuesdays are the public events, *les leçons*. The sole time that you address a crowd other than your peers and students. Hours of memorization in which the drawings you will make are traced, erased, and traced again, until you know that every illustration will be accurate, precise. You rehearse your lecture before me, repeating it so often that I can mouth it back to you like a prompter poised offstage, never needed, this speech of yours fixed flawlessly in your memory. Every detail so conscientiously, so conservatively chosen. Programs printed out and distributed along the aisles, intermissions scheduled upon the hour. And you in the center of the stage. The amphitheatre empty until you order the doors to be opened.

Waiting in the wings, I have counted more than five hundred spectators crowding the circular sweep of seating, spilling into the standing room along the sides, eager to catch a glimpse of *cher professeur*. Gentlemen imitate your dress, your manner, even your monocle, as if hoping to share your illustrious vision. Ladies hand you autograph books to inscribe, leather-bound covers ornamented with gilt.

The interns whisper that there are authors and journalists in the audience, actresses, that the women in furs have performed before royalty. And starstruck, we step onto the boards or find ourselves thrust before the crowd. Those who cannot walk are borne to the stage on stretchers, their bodies stricken and small, swallowed by the immensity of the auditorium. Side by side, we form a living tableau, posed amidst sketches and plaster casts. You refer to us by diagnosis, supplanting our proper names, clothing us in concepts. The aged woman in the feathered hat is Parkinson's; the red-headed woman in the simple frock, epilepsy; and I, spectacular in my flowing night-gown, with the ribbons in my hair, I go by the most majestic name of all, a word strung together from hisses and sighs. *La grande hystérie*.

We possess a museum of living pathology in which the resources are great, you tell the audience. Your finger marking out a frame around us. Your expression for a moment moved, as if you cannot take in the enormity of what you have accomplished. What you have yet to achieve.

Here, at the Salpêtrière, we have converted what was once an arsenal into an anatomo-clinical complex beyond compare—prisons, barracks, clerical quarters subsumed into the body of the institution. But more importantly, you remind them, we have at last separated patients who were housed together indiscriminately, removing the hysterics and epileptics from the population of psychotics and creating a clinic of nervous disorders, what one might refer to as our "new collection."

We are curators who aspire to cure, and we have constructed an appropriately modern institution in which to hold our masterpieces. The hospital grounds are home to endless expansion, innovation—new buildings grafted onto old, kitchens turned into classrooms and clinics, rooms redesigned to accommodate laboratories, studios, electrostatic baths. This is the domain of hystero-epilepsy, of catalepsy, of tetany. The first medical theatre to offer demonstrations on the living. Here, it is the patients who claim our attention, who comprise the exhibits. Standing amongst them, we can almost imagine ourselves inside a hall of statues at Versailles, contemplating the most compelling works of art.

You motion to the rear of the amphitheatre, where a painting hangs of a body bowed backwards like a bridge. Your fingers trace the shape before you, making a flourish so graceful that it is like flight, like a holy gesture—the swing of a censer in church, leaving plumes of smoke braided in air. The figure is lovelier than a body on a cross.

And I think, if there is a Eucharist for this, it is a wafer curved like the roof of the mouth, my tongue curling to taste it—this vaulted and weightless thing, like the ceiling of a cathedral that traps in God.

A single touch sends me to the floorboards, crumpled like a body deprived of breath. A second renders me rigid, taut. The interns lift me onto a gurney, the audience whispering in excitement—anticipating your approach. And then there is no stage, only the sphere around us, the space between us, steadily closing.

You say, seize for me, and place your hands on my stomach, above my hips. Applying gentle pressure, you release and wait, and I, arching my back, ecstatic, pelvis pressing upward, eyes rolling back, teeth gritted, wait for your fingers to find me again. Writhing, rocking, unable to stop, legs twisting around themselves, and the bed hardly beneath me now for more than a moment at a time, as if I am levitating, only my head and my toes touching the mattress. You whisper, *arc-en-ciel*, and the reverence in your voice freezes me there, and I cry out, *Maître*. Everything in focus for a moment.

Each hysteric has her own hysterogenic points, you declare, and it is up to us to discover them, to determine which spots provoke a seizure and which hold the key to its cessation. The patient's body is ever obliging, primed to react to the slightest probing. It is an instrument attuned to our touch. We, in turn, must master the fingerings.

There are critics who object to such inductions, seeking to distinguish between treatment and experimentation. At the Salpêtrière, we draw no such dividing lines. When we stimulate a symptom, we are only recreating that which naturally occurs, in a more suitable setting, within a reasonable timeframe, so that we can observe the phenomenon and postulate a cure. We must remember, *messieurs et mesdames,* in science nothing is gratuitous.

And you, so civilized, so proper when standing before the audience, intend only to grasp my side again, but I twist my torso so that your hand grazes my breast, triggering an attack the likes of which you have never witnessed. Your composure regained so quickly that only I notice it waver.

I improvise on stage, endeavor to exceed your expectations, to make a name for myself. Impressing you with the duration and scope of my attacks, the readiness of my responses. Your dexterous thumb throwing me again and again into seizure. Your modesty easily over-come. Palpating my back, each breast—above, below, and upon the nipple—the back of my knee, my thigh. There, you say, and there. And I on the floor, hoping it will never stop. The spectators lean-ing forward in their chairs. The interns craning their necks to see, mouths open, watching every movement of your hands.

The days are divided into performances, both public and private, interspersed with consults in your study. It is here that patients are presented to you, that attacks develop in darkness. The inner sanc-tum of the study painted black—the walls, the floors, many of the furnishings—obliterating all sense of depth and dimension. The space might stretch on indefinitely or end a few inches behind the massive oak table. It is impossible to tell.

The interns escort us inside, insisting, before we enter, that we pro-duce extraordinary symptoms. Eager to gain credit, to gain favor. They watch possessively each expression on your face, hoping to glimpse approval, pride, respect. You offer sternness—to them, to us, to me.

Intent on observation, you begrudge any interaction. Silent, un-approachable, staring until you have seen enough.

Only in public, in front of a crowd, do you come alive, express awe.

Augustine, you say, looking out at them, your audience, Augustine, and you linger like that over my name, making it hover there above us all so that even I wonder what it is you will make of it, of me, so completely have you taken over that word, Augustine, you say, and we are breathless, all of us, breathless. Your audience waiting for a single utterance from you. Augustine, you say, is the classic example, and we nod, and we let out a sigh. You have said it all so simply, moved us somehow into the realm of art with that one word— *classic*. We are now as those contemplating an exquisite nude—you, the master painter, your hand tracing the anatomical charts, your chin raised, and all of us too somehow raised by your words, the audience suspended several inches above the stage. They look at me, and I look at them, and we look at you, breathless.

You request encores which I willingly perform. I make my entrance like a prop dropped, picked up only at the precise moment it is needed, then indispensable. The focus shifted the moment it is seen.

Note the convex curve of the patient's back, you say, the infamous *arc-en-ciel*. Augustine's form is flawless. First, we are presented with an epileptoid phase with two parts, tonic and clonic, succeeded by elaborately contorted postures—the *attitudes passionelles*, the *poses plastiques*, like an elegant stilled ballet.

At a cursory glance, the attacks seem fragmentary, lacking the least logic or constancy, but nothing could be further from the truth. Look closer and a pattern unravels. Look longer and repetitions emerge. Hysteria has baffled many brilliant minds, convinced the timid to turn back at the very threshold of knowledge, but we walk forward unhesitatingly into its embrace, equipped with every scientific apparatus at our disposal.

Fautes

IN THE LECTURE HALL, he lists symptoms on the blackboard—one below the other, side by side, until the entire board is gridded with them like a word game to be solved—paralysis, hemiplegia, monoplegia, paraplegia, contractures, coxalgia, rhythmic choreas, mutism, stuttering, hiccupping, hysteric anorexia, sensation of strangulation, tachycardia, arrhythmia, precordial pains, polyuria, oliguria, dermographia, urticaria, pathological sweating, erythemas, spasticity, tetany, and pain in the ovaries and abdomen. The acridity of organs.

Hysteria is an illness of imprinting, he tells the interns, etched across the nervous system and the skin. The affliction is pathogenic, endlessly renewing and reproducing itself, spawning concomitant diseases, infecting every appendage, muscle, sensory receptor. It can contort a single finger in contraction or induce a case of tetany that extends from the toes to the innermost workings of the eye. We rely on the patient's consistency, the cyclical nature of her symptoms and seizures, to create a coherent picture of this malady.

He remembers in images rather than words, a *visuel,* closer to painter than *professeur.* Diagramming with voracious eye. Mapping out the dorsal sides, ventral sides, the meridians of spine and breastbone. She watches him draw graphs and charts as if he is an ancient cartographer orienting himself by some unseen set of stars—the spread of hysterogenic points in the dark room as he moves his hands across the plane of her back. Discerning the disparate but distinct frontiers. Marking them with a forefinger, with a thumb.

The interns trail behind him in the ward, compiling lists of sentences he has spoken, reading their notes aloud in front of her as if she can neither hear nor comprehend. They keep track of every body part touched, every gesture performed, but still they cannot decipher the way in which he makes his diagnoses. Until, one day, the bravest among them breaks down in a frustration close to tears and asks him, how? and asks him, why? And dismissively, with an air of impatience, he answers, Why? I cannot tell you why. I know it and that is enough. And as he turns away, she glimpses the students' faces behind his back—sees how they watch him, mystified, as if he possesses second sight.

We must make our way beyond antiquated notions of this disease, he tells the audience. Those that considered the uterus an animated organ that must be kept in place. Such ideas resulted in ludicrous treatments. Physicians would burn bitumen, oil of sulfur, petrol, the hairs of men and goats, the hooves of beasts, shouting into the patient's ears so that she would not faint, pulling out pubic hairs so that the pain excited in the lower regions, the vapor suffocating her, would repulse the womb back into its cavity, whereupon pleasing smells would be introduced into the sex—held open by a spring—in order to soothe the organ into complacency.

The word *hysteria* is symptomatic of a similar conviction, rooted in a womb that has never in fact wandered. So sedentary that we can hold it in our fist, though I will not subject you to such a spectacle.

He picks up a curved metal brace, shaped like the skeletal jaws of a mythical beast, its tongue a whorled screw that tightens as the bolt is turned, clamping down on flesh and viscera.

When we employ uterine compression, our intent isn't to immobilize the womb. We know the application of pressure would work just as well on any hysterogenic point. However, with devices such as the compression belt, which fits around the patient's pelvis, we can pause the attack, relieve her suffering with the smallest turn of a screw.

He lifts her hips slightly, slips the metal mouth in place. And she speaks in tongues then and shakes until her limbs are bruised. Until the belt bites down, preventing any movement. The women in the audience gasping. The men with their hats placed respectfully in their laps.

We cannot rely on familiar contours to guide us, he says. We must consider ourselves explorers of an uncharted interior, provided only with old and misleading maps. For too long, we have clung to crumbling parchments, peering at the tracks of other travelers drawn in broken lines—every gap a hole we might stumble into, every unmarked expanse a discovery waiting to be made. No longer.

We are men creating our own legends, a key of signs and symbols that others can follow. Scientific protocol is the thread we unravel behind us, the path to trace back if ever we are lost.

Each night she pulls her body apart and puts it back together again, and he must discover the places that have irrevocably changed. The subtle ways in which everything must now be realigned. Her neck twisting so violently that her chin comes past her shoulder. Her legs stiffening, feet bent almost backwards.

Her body is a terrain he is certain he can cross. But he finds that there is always something unexpected—the curvature of an ankle, the convulsed and spasmed arm—and realizes that it could take him days to explore. That it could take him years. The lines of longitude and latitude gathered in knots at the base of her bed.

In the intervals between attacks, he makes brief sketches, quick strokes of pen that capture every implausible posture, every anomaly.

Despite his goal of verisimilitude, he cannot resist indulging in artistic touches. Exaggerating the contracture of her shoulders, baring them, as he traces her hair in contours of black lead. Loosening it from its bun so it seeps across the page, a subterranean stream. The straps of the bed erased below her.

Even we find ourselves drawn into an aesthetic, he admits to the audience. In that, there is little shame. Who could fail to be fascinated by this truly prodigious body—brimming with possibilities, with limitless potential.

Merveille

WOMEN LINE THE HALLWAYS FOR MONTHS, gowns pulled down around shoulders, as you document your discoveries, your theorems, your endless experiments. It is no easy task to maintain your attention, to ascertain your fickle moods, your fluctuating interests. Those who reverse their symptoms, who no longer suffer seizures, are returned to the *quartier des aliénées,* where they are left alone. Incurable. Unwatched. And it becomes like a threat whispered throughout the halls. The thought of no longer seeing you. No longer being seen.

So much of this disease can be influenced by suggestion—you explain—by persuasion. The audience nodding in their seats. Me, nodding on the stage. As the body grows more responsive, we hardly need to induce a seizure. Some patients experience fits the moment they step on stage—literally awestruck. Others need only encounter their doctor in the hallway, and they will fall to the floor at his feet. Augustine's renderings are striking in their regularity, practically divided into scenes, acts, *entr'actes,* complete with full intermissions. She seems to control the summoning of her affliction, to parcel it out to us with dramatic precision, with temporal mastery. Some critics see this as a sign of collusion or coercion, but we know better. Hysterics give repeat performances because they cannot do anything else.

They are amateurs, compelled to perform a drama far too grand for them to control.

Once the amphitheatre has emptied and the crowds dispersed, we are lined up one by one, walking the long ward hallways, hands brushing the damp walls. We leave prints behind us—a path of fingers pointing the way to your study. The air filled with the scent of women secreting, of bodies shifting under clamps, under braces. Of moist skin sticking to metal.

Seated behind your desk, you require absolute punctuality. Rising on the stroke of the hour even if I lie before you on the floor. Stepping over me. Gathering your coat and going to the door.

I await the moment when you will end up in front of me and I will give you everything you need, and you will need only me. Augustine, *ma vedette,* you will say, until I become the only patient who enters your *atelier.*

During rounds, the interns induce fits under your supervising gaze, walking through the wards, leaving entire rooms of women delirious, debilitated, tossing in their beds.

I refuse to react to any touch other than your own. Watching the way your eyes move, I act accordingly, crossing and uncrossing my arms, my legs. Moving before you with seamless shifts of hips and shoulders.

In the pauses between attacks, I twist my hair into knots, into carefully constructed buns, wrap myself in ribbons like a gift presented to you—Augustine adorned.

The hysteric makes eyes at her doctors, you tell the audience, treats us like suitors, always eager to misinterpret our gaze, to mistake our professional interest for passion. From its inception, medicine has struggled to define the appropriate distance between doctor and patient, and often it has failed. As physicians, we follow the Hippocratic oath, forbid ourselves "voluptuous enterprises," but even the oath has its mythic origin in a dubious act. Indulge me, if you will, in its retelling.

Hippocrates' first patient was the lovely Avlavia—herself somewhat of a hysteric. The young doctor, a bachelor, couldn't resist his patient's charms—her tired eyes, her graceful swooning body. She was the first living woman whose nakedness he had touched. So modest, and yet at the same time, so ready to reveal herself. He must have recognized inside himself the first stirrings of love, despite the purity of his motives. He sent Avlavia to the oracle of Delphi, desperate for a cure. The oracle told the young woman that her ailment was not fatal, that she could recover by loving and marrying her doctor. Perhaps Hippocrates should have forsworn the oracle's advice, turned the young woman away as she knelt before him, her head bowed. But, as a healer, how could he refuse the patient her cure? What could he do but sanctify the remedy in the holy bonds of matrimony?

Our patients aspire to the same outcome. Augustine is a prime example. At times, she appeals to us with such vulnerability that it seems cruel to reject her affections. She appears to be the embodiment of innocence—stammering, shy, inhibited, so convincing that we can hardly believe she is ill. But woe to him who believes this performance. For he ignores the warning signs at his own risk.

Intermittency is symptomatic of this disease, part of its paradox. We must remain vigilant during such periods of calm, alert to the slightest air of illness—a look in the eye, a strange tilt of the head.

Imagine, if you will, that you are sitting in a garden, gazing at a woman who is composed, peaceful, and a breeze blows by, ruffling her hair, shifting her dress just so, so that when you look at her again, perhaps to doff your hat, you find that the woman has disappeared and another has replaced her—a woman barely kept together, disordered in a way that makes you wary, that makes you drop your gaze and look away, avoiding her eyes, knowing where she will most likely end up: on a bench behind bars, talking to someone who is no longer there—to you perhaps—or wandering the alleyways, chased by children who throw stones, grabbing the scraps of her dress in their hands, tearing until they undo the seams. This is the *aura hysterica,* the premonition that warns you to rise from where you are sitting and walk quickly away.

He who remains will learn soon enough that the patient is no timid virgin. Each attack is an inversion of the coital act—the whole body thrust into an antagonistic arch, a posture both evoking orgasm and exceeding it. The hysteric offers herself as wife and lover, but she is capable of being neither, so she funnels her frustration into symptoms, into the *attitudes passionelles,* professing her passions as if they are destined to be fulfilled, trying to gain pleasure from the gaze, from her fantasy of being at the center of all possible and imaginary desire.

In the amphitheatre, I watch as ladies wave and wink at you, hoping to catch your eye. Perfumed, bejeweled, they are everything that I am not. Extending limp wrists—hands presented to accept a kiss, a bow, a delicate caress. Earrings dangling at their jawlines like tiny, clustered fruit to pluck or suckle.

They are creatures of another species, rarefied and refined. But there is one thing I can offer that they do not possess in endless superlative: the spark that makes the body blaze, flare up, scintillate.

And it is enough—for now—it is everything.

I flirt in front of the audience, place you in compromising positions. Demanding immodest caresses. Each organ corresponding to a different contact point, a varying degree of pressure.

At times, the ease with which you assume predictability irritates me, and I improvise movements you do not expect. Suddenly relaxing or contracting a limb. Presenting a symptom you cannot explain to the audience. I challenge. I cajole. Baring legs and breasts, trying to draw you to me with a look.

The spectators seem to feed off my frustration, faces flushed, as if they too would reach out and touch you, decrease the distance from which you address us—your implacable remove.

And I, rolling an eye, notice the keen and purposeful way in which you focus on a spot slightly above their heads. This habit that betrays unease, allowing you to appear so straightforward, so confident, without ever having to look them in the eye.

Beyond these walls, there would be a life to live. Free from stagecraft and observation. An ordinary life. I can summon no yearning for that existence, no sentimental attachment. I am beyond it now. I have earned my place inside this living museum, as the primary exhibit, the *chef d'oeuvre*. And I am bound here, for good or for ill.

Maladie
1878

HE MARKS THE PASSAGE OF YEARS BY SYMPTOMS ANALYZED. The year of hemiplegia, of aphasia, of hystero-epilepsy. His efforts accumulating accolades, honorary titles, endowments—enabling him to purchase any instruments and embark on any expansion he desires. The crowds grow exponentially. His flock burgeoning into a following, a devout congregation effusive with its praise.

The search for a cure requires a great deal of faith, he tells his disciples, voice brimming with confidence. But his fortune is excessive enough to feel Faustian, dependent upon a bargain he is obligated to fulfill.

In truth, he is astounded at how poorly he understands the ritual he has witnessed unfold each day for years. He can recognize the disease, diagnose and define it, and yet he knows next to nothing about its physiological cause. The ailment able to mimic all maladies at once, to disguise its origins as if it has sprung fully formed from his imagination, a protean monster that continually changes shape.

The harder he tries to verify an infirmity or establish a point of comparison, the more intangible the evidence becomes, forcing him to invent an entire category of pseudo-illnesses—conditions that present identically to actual diseases without any of the accompanying causation. He has witnessed extremities turn necrotic from pseudo-gangrene, organs function to the point of frenzy and then slow to the point of failure for no discernible reason. He has seen patients die from infections that do not appear in their autopsies, and certainly those deaths are not falsehoods. No more than the rare instantaneous recoveries—events that are publicly celebrated and mistakenly ascribed to his abilities.

After the Tuesday demonstrations, witnesses tip their hats and cross themselves before him. Religious weeklies compare his endeavors to the miracles at Lourdes, proclaim him the comforter of his century—the headlines forming a hagiography of sorts, paeans to *le professeur*.

He inhales the admiration like air, lets it fill him, bear him up.

The experts in the audience are not so easily appeased, unwilling to accept a spiritual answer for a scientific dilemma.

Therapeutic marvels are not only part of the natural order of this disease, he tells his peers, they are in fact symptoms. This should not surprise us, since many saints were themselves hysterics, stricken by afflictions that they eventually went on to cure. Hysteria contaminates the true indicators of illness, but that does not mean its existence is false. It has its laws. It has its determinism, like any other disorder. It is not something out of a novel.

We must assume, even though we have not found it, that hysteria does emanate from a lesion of sorts. A dynamic lesion—evasive, changeable, and ever prone to disappear. As coy and ostentatious as the patient herself.

In the amphitheatre, Augustine blends the convulsions of saints with the spasms of sinners, miming crucifixion. Stigmata blushing her palms, her soles. She challenges the figurative nature of every meta-phor—the hematomas so vivid that she truly resembles a martyr im-paled at wrist and ankle, a zealot bleeding and suffering for her god. Sometimes he wishes her perpetual manifestations would cease—ease the mounting pressure to divine meaning from movements that seem increasingly meaningless. Her body on stage a provocation that demands a response.

Off stage, she is no less insistent—clamoring for his attention, growing petulant and preoccupied when she senses his discontent, her pathology increasing rather than abating.

He seeks sanctuary in the *amphithéâtre d'autopsie*, in the quiet preci-sion of corpses. Cadavers watching with glazed eyes as cuts are made, tumors excised, lobes of the brain exposed. The bodies lie on cold steel slabs, fluids drained into troughs below. Congealed blood. Bile. The contents of the bladder. Nothing remains concealed here. In the frigid air, breaths coalesce into vapors, tiny clouds that dissipate quickly, though few are released to trouble the air. On a table, a se-quence of vertebrae helix into a tortuous spine, each bone boiled and gleaming, the marrow removed. Nearby, a brain rests on a scale, the crenulated folds crowned by a massive, fibrous clot. Cerebral fluid filling the scale's bowl like a glistening, crystalline lake.

He can lose himself for hours in the minutiae of anatomy, the burden of time temporarily alleviated as he focuses on flesh that is preserved from perishing. In her presence, he is painfully aware of years elapsing. No longer a young man, he cannot help but note his declining physique—the decrease in muscle tone, the whitening hair. The inverse proportion of time allotted to accomplishments sought.

∽

He stands before the audience, hands clasped, head lowered, in the attitude of a penitent or a man confessing. Let us be honest, he says. Any scientist, if offered the choice, would extricate himself from the mess and corruption of the corporeal, would traffic solely in the realm of ideas. We do not relish our servitude to the flesh, our dependence on our patients. On the contrary, we long for an unfettered existence, a life of transcendence. Yet this is a choice denied to us.

This disease forces us to delve deeper in search of mastery, of expertise—down to the very bone if need be. Many who stand outside the medical field consider dissection distasteful. Some go as far as to declare it sacrilegious, but who is to say that the hands of the pathologist are any less reverent than those of the priest, that anatomy is not its own sacred enterprise? Christianity loves its martyrs, revels in the mortification of their flesh almost more than in the ascension of their spirit. Why should we, who also serve a higher good, abstain from these iconic bodies which would be crowning pieces in any scientific reliquary?

He wheels a cadaver out onto the amphitheatre stage, exposing an atrophied muscle and pointing to Augustine's convulsed leg, trying to draw parallels between the living tissue and the dead. Yet her movements interfere with any meaningful comparison, the complexity of her dynamism overshadowing the grey, inert matter extracted with forceps and tongs.

He can feel the lack of enthusiasm among the lay audience, the crowd's failure to comprehend—after the initial shock and nausea— the grandeur of morbid anatomy. And he senses in this slight misstep the first of many to come. Frustrated that he must rely on substitutes, women who have predeceased her. Wishing it was her body beneath his scalpel, stiffening below the blade.

∾

Lately, I can find no pose to please you, my unhappy *Maître*, my displeased *professeur*.

When you approach me on stage, it is with a look of distraction, detachment. The same gaze that greets me inside your study as you point to a spasm, to the curve of my back, but without reverence. Without awe. The arc of every limb grown tiresome.

Weeks pass without you asking for a single seizure. Your voice impatient and strident, cutting through the edges of things. From below, your face appears as a collection of angles: your beaked nose, your chiseled brow, sharp enough to inflict injury.

You spend more time with corpses than you do with me. Pouring over anatomical charts and data in your study, coming out only to confirm a symptom or consider an incision point.

In the amphitheatre, you recite a corporal geography that I learn by heart: the thoracic inlet, the pelvic brim, the lozenges of Aphrodite. Behind you, diagrams of a body stripped of skin, the plush red muscles that clothe it from head to foot. You explain how to detach tendons, cut nerves, expose organs, marking dissection lines with the tip of your finger, elucidating the difficulty of cleanly separating skin from musculature, how the two seem to cleave together, threaded with fibers, veins, and fascia. The latticework like the lace of a bridal veil.

From the pulpit, you address your congregation—the crowd fixated, their faces rapt. You say, our relationship with the afflicted is a marriage of sorts, a union until death, born of the flesh, bound by the body. Or perhaps, to be more precise, it is a perpetual betrothal, secured by the tantalizing promise of eventual penetration. After all, the autopsy creates an intimacy that is closer to consummation than any comparable act.

I stop listening, repeat the phrases *marriage, union, betrothal, consummation* inside my head. Your words all that have sustained me for months now.

I have learned more about my condition from what you've said to others than from a single sentence ever spoken to me directly. Sessions spent standing on the stage like a player in a parlor game, a prognosis scrawled on a sheet of paper and affixed to my person, somewhere out of sight. A secret phrase that I must try to determine while you supply clues and code words to the audience, trying not to give the answer away.

I have learned even less about you—scraps overheard in the hallways, morsels scavenged from your clenched jaws. I know that you live amidst a menagerie of animals, surrounding yourself with species that are dear to you. When you speak about the fragrant paws of dogs, the way in which a bird's feather when pulled back on itself is even softer underneath than it is above, when you speak of these things, you become radiant, *Maître.* Your face growing unguarded. And I think that you must be human after all, capable of adoration. But the impulse is seldom aroused, despite my best intentions.

One day, I pass you in the courtyard stooped over a sparrow that has collided with a windowpane. You cup it in your palm, careful not to startle it too severely; its chest palpating like an eyelid in the midst of a fever dream. You croon and chirr to it under your breath, assuring me that it is only dazed. As if I too fear for its life. But, *Maître,* I have other fears, seek other assurances.

You pass the tiny, twitching body to me—our hands touching during the transfer, the pulse of a heart momentarily clasped in our palms—and I am moved by this gesture of trust, your faith that I will not crush it.

I would transform myself if I could, drape myself in fur or feathers, become bird or beast for you. I would ruffle my wings or raise my hackles so you could smooth them again. I would stun myself in order to make you stare into my eyes, to watch your ecstatic expression as my body stirred once again in response to the benevolence of your touch.

I have endured this public courtship patiently—accepted, for the most part, its formalities and limitations. All at your insistence. But how can passion withstand such a prolonged engagement, with every interaction supervised and every expression of intimacy so profoundly restrained?

At times I wonder if there is any part of you that wants a living wife. You show no hint of appetite, of arousal, as I sit before you, my hand between my legs, neck thrown back. The cold snap of metal and your fingers even colder. It is as if I have lost you before I have even had you. Your patience used up, your interest. Then something shifts, and I note the darkening of your eyes when you witness beauty, when you cannot look away. Emotions expressed in increments so slight as to seem imagined seconds after they pass.

All I ask is to be your paramour, your partner. I have opened myself up to you, *Maître*. I have welcomed you under my skin. And I'm not sure how much longer I will deign to wait.

Relief

IN CHARCOT'S DREAM, Augustine poses before him, her head coated in plaster, her body naked. From certain angles, the paste blends into the whiteness of the wall, so that she resembles a sculpture beheaded on the stage.

He removes the mask roughly, ignoring the raw appearance of her newly revealed flesh, the way she winces at the light. She instinctively touches her cheeks—expecting, perhaps, to feel the slickness of sebum. Touching instead the cool reassurance of skin. He looks away, avoiding the intensity of her relief, startled to see that the faces in the audience are blank, unresponsive.

The hysteric's body produces innumerable *objets d'art*, he proclaims, sweeping his arm toward a display of casts and moldings arranged on the far side of the stage—the limbs familiar but impersonal, a refuse pile of unneeded appendages. He places her plaster visage beside them, angled on the table so that it watches him from across the room. Two more eyes trained upon him. Two more ears listening to his voice. No sooner has he put it down and walked away than he turns around, picks it up again, tempted for a moment to nestle his face behind the mask, to peer at her from behind her own lids. To see her through her own eyes.

Even after he wakes, he cannot stop picturing the casts, their simplistic, toneless contours, their pristine lack of flesh.

The dead are limited in what they can teach us, he tells the audience, his voice shaken. How are we to verify a hysteric's muscular contracture if we cannot open her arm at the moment of paralysis and glimpse the tissue and fiber? How can we observe the effect of the brain's anatomy upon the patient's thoughts and actions? In an ideal world, we would practice vivisection. But one cannot descend into the body's interior without consequence, without potential calamity.

Where does that leave us? Are we destined only to examine surfaces—to touch, but never deeply, never conclusively, upon the enigma of the disease? Surely not, he says, steadying his voice. Surely, we cannot abide such limitations.

We must resign ourselves to the cultivation of patience. We let the disease unravel, progress to its end, and we learn from it. From its steady march toward death. A dalliance, you might say, with a state of disaster.

Gratification cannot forever be deferred in the face of the incurable. Eventually, we shall claim our prize. And then, like augurs, we will scrutinize the intestines for signs, split the body open, autopsy the remains. Until that time, we must seek other means of access.

The woman on the bed is almost all bone. Too weak to move herself, she fractures when she touches the bedframe even slightly. Her mouth open. Her deformed knees unbearable to behold. When the interns come at night, their white coats bright in the sleeping room, they kneel at her bedside, and her expression never changes. Eyes always open, she never seems to sleep. The interns have brought buckets filled with white paste. They cover her slowly like painters preparing a canvas—coating her, head to toe, until she is luminous.

I hide in a corner of the room—an unseen set of eyes, a witness. I check myself for fractures, feel the constriction of the cast as if it is covering me. My body so rigid I can no longer move.

You arrive late, *Maître*, checking your pocket watch, watching as the woman's shallow breast, her neck, her face is covered, and she coughs. Sputtering. Spitting paste from her mouth. Choking. You do nothing to assist her. When the interns are done, they crack the covering off her and carefully, next to the bed, place her twin, an exact duplicate—the sticklike legs, the hollow of every rib, the flattened nipples. They remove it from the room under your ever-watchful eyes. As the woman in the bed, rolling feebly, breaks another bone—the fracture spreading blue across her skin—deserted by that pale other who does not break so easily, moving still and ghastly through the halls and into your study.

It is there when I enter again. It is there ever after. And the brittle woman becomes increasingly irrelevant to you—an emaciated antique amidst the carefully selected décor.

When the interns come for me, I refuse to comply, clinging to the bedframe, digging my heels into the floor. They carry me, thrashing, through the hallways to the *atelier de moulage*, bolt me into a set of braces, then depart. The castings, propped against walls and tables, survey me with marbled eyes—an audience of absent bodies and forged limbs. On the floor are a number of long wooden boxes holding within them full-length plaster molds—the shapes of patients impressed in the negative space. It is rumored that cadavers are carried into the sculpture studio at night, positioned like animate bodies. But there are only replicas here. Replacements.

I will not sit for a casting, exhorting the interns that I have much more to offer *in vivo*, insisting that they bring you to me and allow me to explain. Instead I am left in the empty studio for days on end. And time seems to harden and congeal, to take on an infinite, unvaried pallor. Nothing can withstand this vacuity—thought is negated, speech devoured. It is as if the world itself has been unmade.

Only the restraints stop me from pulling the veins from my arms, like weeds uprooted, ready for the plucking. And one thing becomes clear. When I am not looked at, I do not exist. When I am not touched, I am without a body.

Surely something exists only if there is someone to see it.

Weeks pass before you return to the studio. When I see you, I detail a list of indignities, shouting accusations at the interns, who speak to you as if I am not even in the room. I cannot imagine that you have condoned their behavior, but soon it is obvious that you will brook no dissent from me. Your face severe, a sharp composition.

I know I have displeased you, *Maître,* by refusing to cooperate, but I cannot bear the idea of encasement. I prefer to sit in the corner, ignored, forgotten. Grateful at least to have the comfort of companionship. Resolved to find another way to return to your good graces.

The interns fetch patients from the wards, and I watch as the women pose for the moldings. They sit demurely as you pour the plaster, sculpt the wax—copies of themselves emerging virgin, unblemished, their skin moist and pliant. You work intently on each figure, etching out the features. Attention paid to every pore as you bend supple limbs to stiffness.

They take my place upon the stage. These still, white others. With their sealed lips, their closed eyes. Their infinite ability to hold a pose.

One statue in particular earns your attention. *Une jeune mademoiselle.* Displaying, as she does, so exquisitely, the hyperflexion of joint and spine. She returns from the amphitheatre with an air of smugness, an aura of adulation clinging to her. There is no denying the sculpture's allure. Beside her, I am an awkward understudy, un-prepped and unneeded.

It is a matter of concentration, of endurance, as I emulate her exactitude, imagine knitting muscle into bone. Grimacing as my body betrays me time and time again. Twitching, quivering, wrenching into knots. I do not resist the pain; I become it. Biting my tongue so I will not vomit, blood collecting at the back of my throat.

I imagine myself corseted, envision a binding that maintains my posture. And gradually I feel my sinew crackle like plaster. My circulation slowed to torpor, turning my skin etiolated and cold.

When the interns enter the *atelier*, they do not recognize me, so closely have I mimicked *les autres*, so complete is my transformation. They carry me at last into the amphitheatre, setting me down beside a row of casts.

The sculptures and I sit side by side, before the audience. We span the stage like a chain of paper dolls, deceptively delicate, convincingly calm.

Even when she resists us, the patient succumbs to predictability, you tell the crowd. What is amazing—wondrous even—is our ability to mold her, to shape her responses to given events, to predetermined stimuli. Surround her with statues, and she becomes a statue.

That which we underestimate is hysteria's prodigious pace. How swiftly Augustine masters the imitative art! How deftly she mimics the moldings on the stage! Her eagerness is quite useful, as far as we are concerned. It advances the progress of our studies, allows us to examine the most extraordinary phenomena almost at will.

Contracture is one of these phenomena. Note the patient's intertwined arms, the tucked position of her head, so indicative of convulsion, yet devoid of movement. This is the classic quality of tetanism. Though blood still flows to the muscles, the limbs freeze to the point of fixity, rigor mortis. In this state, the body is almost invincible.

You pull at my arms, try to untwist them. I do not resist, put no effort into maintaining the position, angered at how easily you have taken it for granted. Nevertheless, my limbs remain interlaced. And I realize then how malleable you have made me, how thoroughly I have underestimated your skills.

You have manipulated me without a touch, more easily than if I'd been made of clay.

Your fingers dig into the skin, leaving marks that will surely form bruises, yet I feel nothing. Any more pressure, you say with a grunt, and the bones will shatter.

You release your grasp, but I do not attempt to move—afraid of what may fragment, shear off like a chunk of granite from its base. I could not shift a muscle now by any force of will. Not even a tremor disturbs the surface, arrested in its raging stillness.

We can invoke this condition for our benefit, you explain. What is our leverage? The answer, *messieurs et mesdames*, is, in a word, attention.

Attendez-moi. The hysteric lacks the most basic sense of interiority, feels instead a consuming emptiness, an absence of identity akin to death. For this reason, she will go to extraordinary lengths to avoid abandonment, complying with demands that are contrary to her physical well-being.

For the patient, tetanism is a harrowing impasse—the body locked in battle with itself, refusing to yield. The result is nothing short of excruciation. Try to sit still, truly still, for more than several minutes, and you will quickly understand the devastating power of muscles and nerves, their ability to inflict injury. All this, the hysteric endures to avoid isolation. Her body petrifies itself.

Her quiescence provides us with an ideal condition for casting. We cannot ignore this advantage. We cannot fail to exploit it. Instead, we mix the plaster and go to work.

It occurs to me that I am defenseless, that my body has immobilized me better than any brace. I can only appeal to your mercy, silently beg for a reprieve.

The interns spread a tarp out beneath me to protect the wooden slats of the stage from any spatter, setting a bucket on top, just inside the range of my peripheral vision. You turn to face me, and for a moment you recognize my terror. And something softens in your gaze, slightly, before you look away.

In such a state, you muse—half to yourself, half to the audience, the hint of a smile settling around your mouth—we could have our way with the patient, overcome every resistance.

Augustine, for example, displays a particular reluctance to being cast, especially in a full-body mold. In fact, her refusal borders on dread, akin perhaps to the fear of being buried alive.

We need not indulge her fears, nor allow her the satisfaction of dictating how we proceed. But, we are not sadists here, you proclaim like a judge granting a stay of execution. We will spare her and rely on her to repay the favor.

Rather than emerging empty-handed, we will make molds of her extremities. After hours spent in these improbable positions, the harm cannot be particularly great.

As I watch, your expression becomes beatific—the face of a man at peace, at least for the moment. His mission God-given and indisputable, his righteousness reaffirmed. It is hard not to feel awe, to bask in the divinity of your mercy. You look down at me once more and a shudder of gratitude passes through my body—the only evidence of movement to come over me in hours—so profound is my sense of relief, of appreciation.

You take my hand to prepare it for the plaster. It lays curled and crippled in the center of your palm until you place your other hand on top of it—creating a cradle that comforts and protects—holding it there as the fingers twitch and spasm and slowly unclench. Numbness giving way to warmth. The sensation of skin on skin.

I slip my fingers between yours, enlace them, and you do not pull away. Our palms pulsing, as if you have opened my dress, slid your fingers over my breast, into my ribcage, and grasped my heart.

The tremors spread to my face, my eyes closing involuntarily, narrowing the world until you are my only point of contact. And when you speak it sounds like your voice is inside me, your breath is my breath, your words nestled in the hollows of my ears.

In our treatment of this disease, you say so softly that the seats creak as the crowd strains to hear you, we assent to a contract of sorts, a grand bargain both sacred and profane. We perform an act of faith-healing that depends on the patient's confidence in her doctor, her unwavering conviction in his power. No matter what we ask of her, in one way or another we attain her consent.

In turn, we accept her collaboration as a gesture of good faith—perhaps, even, as an offering of some deeper attachment. For what is consent if not the lowering of all barriers, the abandonment of one's very being? It is the basis of servitude, torment, torture. But more than that, it is the manifestation of unconditional love, a complete dispossession of the self in order to be possessed by the other. Such belief makes miracles manifest, as our patients surrender to our ministry, entrust us with their very souls.

I open my eyes and smile. My facial muscles contorting as if my cheeks have been sliced open. And a shock passes through you as you recognize your first completely accurate observation—the magnitude of my feelings for you. This *grand mal,* and the burden it bestows.

II.

Exposures
1879

THE INTERNS LEAD ME INTO A ROOM with walls built of opaque glass, heavy curtains drawn to block out the light. Placed on a platform, I am unsure what is expected of me. The air dense with anticipation, with a sense of imminence. Only after my eyes adjust do I see it— the magnificent bed—situated amidst lights and backdrops in the center of the room. And I think, they have brought me here for you, *Maître,* to this nuptial bed, which they tuck and plump, ready for our consummation.

I eye it like an eager bride and climb in readily, adopt a pose and wait. Nearly an hour passes without your arrival, and I begin to panic.

The interns reach behind me and unfold a headrest and iron supports. Patience, they say, he is on his way. Slipping my limbs into hidden braces and scrupulously concealed clamps, draping them in folds of cloth.

But when you enter the room at last, you are not alone. And I ask, *Monsieur,* what is this, gesturing nervously to the box wheeled before me—its glassed eye staring like your monocled lens, but empty. No iris, no pupil—like an eye rolled back to whiteness, unblinking. Your hand caressing the wood, the metal, the accordioned back. And you say, Augustine. But I do not hear the rest, the box between us clicking loud enough to drown out a reply.

We spend hours in this replica of a bedroom, the apparatus sitting beside you like a strange mechanical man—a colleague with whom you are conversing, heads bowed close together, whispering conspiratorially. Watching me from the back of the room, you seem farther away than ever, a critic appraising the production, evaluating the *mis-en-scène.* The bed a prop in which I lie alone.

I find myself unable to perform, stricken with a self-consciousness approaching stage fright. I await cues that do not come, listen for prompts whispered through pursed lips, but the backdrop is blank, barren of clues—the box a theatre I cannot see inside. Your countenance hidden behind its curtain.

From the edge of the bed, I reach out to you, request that you join me. Promising to produce wonders if only you will emerge from behind the apparatus, lay your hands on me. I say, let me see your face, *Maître.* Without it, there is nothing human in this room.

The photographic studio is the eye of the asylum, he announces. For every corporeal fascination, we have created a new *atelier*—an anatomy lab in which to hold limbs in our hands, a museum in which to display the bones, a gallery of moldings. But nothing, *mesdames et messieurs,* nothing is comparable to this.

With the camera we can see and stop any movement, capture the slightest contortion, the fits that occur even in the middle of the night when you and I are not around to witness them. In a way, you could say that the studio is an amphitheatre of a different sort, with an audience that is far more attentive—for nothing can lull the technological eye to sleep. It is an implacable observer, unswayed by sentiment, immune to emotion—detecting details that would otherwise go undiscerned.

Observation is the oldest scientific undertaking. Let us recall the seminal myth of madness, born of the disastrous marriage between Zeus and Hera, king and queen of the gods. It begins, like so many Greek myths, with the discovery of adultery. Learning that her husband has impregnated Semele, princess of Thebes, Hera spreads rumors that the girl is inventing a lie to cover up her promiscuity. The goddess adopts the guise of a trusted nursemaid and convinces Semele to restore her reputation by confirming her lover's immortal identity. The princess is persuaded. She insists that Zeus visit her in his full and terrible splendor, binding him with a vow on the river Styx. But the moment he enters the girl's bedchamber, his radiance consumes her, splitting her open from sex to scalp like a bolt of lightning. Zeus snatches the half-formed fetus from the smoldering ashes, slicing a gash in his thigh and enfolding the child inside. He harbors it secretly in this flesh-made-womb, through gestation until unnatural birth. And thus the world is delivered the deity Dionysus. The child grows up to become god of the vine—Bacchus—cultivator of intoxication and delirium, worshipped by thousands, followed by legions of ecstatic women. Everywhere he travels, maidens flock to join these wild-eyed maenads, wreathing their hair in ivy, draping their forms in fawn skins that they tear from steaming carcasses during the height of drunken bacchanals.

Thus, the scene is set. Ripe for a reckoning.

As Euripides recounts, Dionysus returns—vengeful—to the city of Thebes, the site of his conception, of his mother's immolation, to find himself and his rituals scorned, his godhead denied, his mother mocked as a liar and whore. Youthful and stubborn King Pentheus has ordered the Bacchic ceremonies banned and their leader arrested. The king ignores all importunities for caution, piety—enraged that the women of the city have taken to the countryside, inebriated and raving, led by his own mother, Agave. Rather than soften the young ruler's resolve, Dionysus assumes the identity of the shackled prisoner, leader of the Bacchae, in order to goad the king to greater outrage, to stoke his desire to watch the maniac women perform their sacred, secret rites. Dionysus smites Pentheus with delusions, with a veil of madness. And so the king garbs himself in maenad's robes, adopts a womanish manner, and climbs into a pine tree to observe his mother and her handmaids.

We, *messieurs et mesdames,* know all too well what spectacles awaited him there, what troubling visions. For we too have seen them, and now we are poised to reveal them.

We need not fear the play's calamitous finale: the watcher discovered and torn from the trees, hunted down by his mother, who saw in her god-addled eyes not a son but a lion to be slain and dismembered, his head carried back in triumph—her pride turned to torment as soon as her frenzy passed.

We are not living a tragedy. There is no vengeful god awaiting his chance to betray us.

We are scientists faced with nothing less than the opportunity to bring an entirely new methodology into existence—anatomo-clinical photography: the experimental, pedagogical, and archival use of the camera in medicine. Photography gives us the power to become progenitors and patriarchs of an artform, to depict madness in all its infinite variations via a purely objective medium. We can move beyond hand-drawn diagrams and depictions. We can conduct thorough examinations without relying on castings and autopsies. And most importantly, we can at last dispense with the imprecision of language, description, the need for eloquence to mediate and convey what we see.

There is one caveat, of course: the camera is only as effective as the man who wields it. The apparatus must be set up and focused to take a picture the moment the collodion plate is prepared, any exposure occurring before the plate has dried. For that reason, the physician has to detect the subtlest indications of impending upheaval if he is to capture the *aura hysterica* passing across the patient's countenance. He cannot let down his guard, allow himself to be distracted, lest he miss the shot.

No matter how quickly he reacts, her seizures cease the moment she is placed before the camera. Her body slouching into a seated pose, limbs limp and lifeless. She resembles an automaton whose internal mechanism has broken, gears interlocking.

During such extended intermissions, he struggles to make use of her stillness. Biding his time by creating some semblance of the mundane. He unbuckles the remaining straps of the *camisole de force*—which is, after all, irrelevant now—replacing the straitjacket with a bodice of metal braces that holds her upright. Pulling a coarse wool dress over her head, he buttons it up to her throat, hiding the supports. He ties a black ribbon around her neck before sliding hooks through the holes in her ears and letting the earrings dangle halfway to her throat. Gathering her wild hair in his hands, he twists it into a tight, unwilling bun. A few strands escape to curl around her earlobes. He props her head against her hand, secures it with a clamp, her elbow leaning casually on the back of the chair. Her other hand placed docilely in her lap.

He will use this picture in his lectures to represent her "normal state," the starting point of her disease. He envisions a series of photographic tableaux burgeoning from this single image, an array of seizures and poses branching outward like a complex genealogy—revealing the roots of hysteria, establishing a hierarchy of symptoms. A catalogue replete with photographic plates, intricate explanations, the answers to innumerable questions. His masterpiece. Its existence still a seed in his mind—nurtured and carefully guarded, but quickening.

The moment the photographic apparatus is removed, her body resumes its motion—agonized, as limbs that have remained immobile suddenly flail and convulse, jerk into action. She swoons, overturning the chair in which she sits, tearing the earrings from her ears. He rushes to restore the straitjacket, to restrain her, all resemblance lost between one image and the next.

In the months that follow, the disease resists him at every turn—producing movement when he seeks immobility, stasis when he craves progress. He equips the amphitheatre with projection machines, hoping to divert the audience with the latest inventions and innovations. But he is careful to ensure that Augustine cannot see her likeness, uncertain of the effect it might have on her.

He displays the photograph of her *état normale* on a screen above the stage, the audience transfixed, unable to account for its banality when juxtaposed with the fury of her fits. He uses the dissonance to his advantage, keeps the crowd confounded, sending her into extravagant seizures while her portrait watches serenely from above.

For the patient, the onset of an attack is anything but subtle, he says. It begins with a burning sensation in every extremity, muscles twisting and retracting, so that her walk, her gestures unfold in erratic disarray. It becomes an effort to make even the simplest motion, and gradually she stops trying, born down by some staggering and central fatigue, her ears buzzing, her limbs heavy. As soon as she allows herself to be still, she is struck by a blast, rushing upwards, as if a central rupture has occurred. Her speech cut off, her gaze wandering, she suffers from pounding headaches, shrill noises echoing inside her eardrums. She cringes at the slightest touch.

He points to the projection, feels the attention of the audience shift with him—as if the crowd is one being with many eyes—and suddenly he is filled with a feeling of unease, a performance anxiety that he has worked hard to overcome but has never fully mastered. He stands outside himself, watching himself speak, hearing every word he utters twice, the syllables overlapping until he cannot recognize the words. His vision doubles and the foreground flattens alarmingly, the stage suddenly pitched and angled, precarious. And now there are four Augustines, two audiences, and far too many eyes. It is all he can do to pull himself together, to wrench the familiar world back into being, but he does so—gathering his breath, focusing on a single spot on the wall until his nerves calm. He knows from experience that no one is likely to have detected anything amiss. However, even without looking at her, he can sense the renewed intensity with which Augustine watches him. And he knows he has not escaped her notice. That she has seen through his disguise.

The hysteric wears many faces, many masks, he continues, his composure solidifying as the fragmented images knit themselves back into one. The physician's task is to reveal this age-old drama as it unfolds: peering from behind the camera, trying to glimpse the performance, to render the scene.

He is relieved every time he receives an ovation—the applause of the audience a buttress boosting him up, sustaining the weight of his speculations. Yet his apprehension remains. The live presentations are a perilous undertaking—too novel to the medical field to constitute proof, too stunning to escape scrutiny. He is out on a limb without enough photographic evidence to support his presumptions, each demonstration requiring him to strike a delicate balance, to elicit amazement without inciting doubt. He is well aware that even the most suitable staging can shift from artful to artificial in the audience's eye. That, once lost, credibility cannot easily be recovered.

Daily, he scours the pages of periodicals for scholars who challenge his authority or level allegations of subterfuge, determined not to let any criticism take root. But the first tendril appears in a publication of note, passed around by the interns, discussed in hushed whispers before he gets ahold of it. Planting spores and seedlings in fertile soil.

Is it not possible, the author asks, that there is some sort of chicanery going on? Theatre, *par excellence*, in which the actresses truly embody their roles and execute them under expert direction? How can a disease be considered legitimate if no organic marker has been found? If fevers prove false and syndromes repeatedly reveal themselves as "pseudos" without measurable veracity? In the few photographs published to date of the Salpêtrière's star performer, we can hardly believe that an attack is taking place; the straitjacket that appears in one photograph offers our only indication that something is wrong. Even that she wears like a whalebone corset, comporting herself so that we nearly forget to notice it. In light of these discrepancies, must we not ask ourselves if the patient dissembles on stage, if she has been schooled in the art of deception?

Révélateur

ONE EVENING YOU SUMMON ME TO THE STUDIO, unusually late, the interns absent, the lamps dimmed.

The camera glares from a corner of the room—a chaperone disturbed from sleep, plotting future punishments. I assume my customary position, seated on the edge of the bed like any ordinary woman, legs crossed, arms folded, unexceptional. Waiting for you to take your place behind the veil.

Instead, you join me on the platform, reach inside your breast pocket and pull forth a silvered phial crafted from mercury glass, its stopper angled and faceted, lachrymal. You uncork an elixir and instruct me to inhale, passing the bottle under my nose—the sharp odor more penetrating than any perfume.

And then the camera disappears and the room dissolves around us. Your eyes fixed upon mine, as if our gaze has fused. From nowhere, you produce a paintbrush, your hand moving sinuously to create a series of luminous brushstrokes. Line by line, you compose a nude, the paint clinging to the air as if there is a canvas between us, its weave too delicate to see. With each stroke, a limb takes shape before me, a contour that I recognize as my own. Fleshed out to the point that I can feel the nerves sensitize, enliven, the sensations transferred to my skin so that I experience them simultaneously. Each body part numb until you paint it, create it in the air, conjure it into existence. The bristles of the brush tracing my collarbone, my nipples, my belly, dipping down into the dark space between my thighs, the cleft of my buttocks—shaping me from the inside out. You depict a limb in a particular pose and my own limb moves to match it. My body restored to motion with a flick of your wrist. I watch your expression become almost ecstatic, your muscles clenched, your hand trembling. And I stare at you wide-eyed, in absolute awe.

The next morning, the sunlight in the amphitheatre makes me squint—every object too clearly defined, every edge too obvious. I crave a purely nocturnal existence. The fumes still heavy on my breath, seeping from my pores. If I could, I would inhale them anew. Instead, I fidget through your lecture, skin itching, muscles aflame.

We can minister drugs directly to the patient, you tell the crowd, either through inhalation, ingestion, or injection, in order to precipitate hysterical vertigoes and inebriations, to witness the effects of different stimulants upon the attacks. We have at our disposal a veritable pharmacopeia of morphines and chlorohydrates, sulphates and atropines. With all the substances in our possession, the intoxication need never cease.

I show you in hours what it once took me days to unfold. The stillness dissipating like a vapor—vanishing as unexpectedly as it arrived. The camera gathers my movements in a single glance. My limbs blurring in their efforts to enthrall. I ask you, *Maître*, how am I to compete? As you offer me your hand, lead me to the bed, give me a rag to breathe, and the glass eye becomes a mirror before which I primp and preen, twist my body into the most elaborate arcs and knots. Hips thrusting against empty air.

You move with alacrity, placing powder on my tongue to agitate my movements, inserting needles into my veins to induce languor or increase lability. Your brusque manner softening with each act of collaboration, as my body grows accustomed to the rhythm of the lens, the way it devours.

I test your patience, requesting rouge and makeup, fussing endlessly over my appearance. I instruct the interns in the art of *maquillage,* captivate them with the deftness of my fingers, distract them. Until you usher them impatiently out of the studio, and do not ask them to return.

Another picture, another pose, a costume change, and behind the screens, the background shifts cunningly, but I see only your face, attentive, focused, as I move my arms outward to begin a bow.

In the studio at night, when no one is watching, you indulge in unorthodox experiments, private sessions that leave me mesmerized. A watch dropped in front of my eyes. A pen moved slowly back and forth. And then, *Maître,* your hands become a source of entrancement, making objects materialize out of emptiness—a pear I can cup in my palm, a wick of flame—reeling out a skein of visions.

Outside the door, the row of patients dwindles daily, flattening into representations of themselves—their pale bodies pressed to the dark walls like paintings. As if a séance has been performed here. The afterglow of apparitions seared into the woodwork.

You say, Augustine, and your voice echoes through the hallway each evening, beckoning me to the studio—but of this I cannot be sure. A name uttered here might just as easily be an echo of the camera's click, a reverberation of the shutter. Nevertheless, the sound is

enough to lure me past the threshold, where space expands and contracts around fluctuating levels of light.

I wait for the slightest movement of screens to announce your
presence, to shift and reveal you, uncover the corner in which you
sit watching. Never knowing from which entrance you will emerge
and with what accompaniment—illuminated or eclipsed, raucous
or silent. Some nights, I walk into a room alive with music—the
clashing of cymbals, of bells, the beating of tympani drums. Sometimes a gong strikes close to my ear and the sound deafens me,
freezing me in place until the spark of a flash moves me again.

The discharge of radiance forms a halo above your head, obscuring your face like that of a pagan god too resplendent to behold. Its
aura enfolding you, enfolding us both. And I say, *Maître, mon dieu.*
Lifting my hands in exultation.

Some nights, you cannot take your eyes from me, whispering *extraordinary* and *Augustine* as if you cannot tell the words apart.

You say, Augustine, your name is like a flower unfurling, and
you bring forth shining glass balls like those used by sailors to trap
witching spirits, revolving mirrors borrowed from the bird catcher,
magnets curved delicately in the middle of your palm. You ignite
glittering filaments, the beams spinning and scattering, catching in
the antique looking glasses that line the walls, ensnaring me amidst
reflections. Your many heads, your multiple eyes, staring from countless corners. The room become faceted, crystalline, each surface
fractured and cleaved.

You are everywhere. You fill this small space entirely. My vision
doubling until I can no longer distinguish flesh from refraction, trying to lure your reflection from the glass, to discover the angle of the
prism that will press me up against my mirror-*maître*. And I think, I

will do anything you ask, the beams spinning in so many directions at once.

Augustine, you say to me, Augustine, and I do not even know what the word you utter means.

∽

She falls into spells of enthrallment so complete they approach dispossession. His every suggestion imbued with the power of commandment, so that she sees what he tells her to see, feels what he tells her to feel, without resistance or recoil. The initial occurrence entirely accidental, fortuitous—the inhalations combining unexpectedly with light and movement to elicit an impromptu state of hypnosis. Her mobility before the lens a miraculous side effect after so much stillness—allowing, at last, an opportunity to photograph the entirety of the attack, each *érotisme, extase, supplication amoureuse*. Surely he is obliged to investigate, he tells himself, despite the stigma attached to such pseudo-science.

He adds secret late-night sessions to his schedule, documenting them with photographs that he develops himself. Augustine the only eyewitness, her gaze cast upward, observing phantasms that do not exist—illusions in ether-laden air.

In his study, he trims and edits the photographs, assigns them captions, numbers, and titles. Making sure that the braces and stands are erased from view, that the straps of straitjackets are whited over with gouache, retouched. That he himself is never captured within the frame.

He amasses a record of gestures and moods evoked under hypnosis, a veritable thesaurus of somnolent expressions. Surprise, delight, disdain, pouts, threats, ecstasy. Adding page after page to the collection he plans to publish.

Often, he labors straight through to morning. The interns pacing past his office, too intimidated to knock. A thick aura of silence surrounding any room that he is in. They say, *le Maître* is working, and whisper amongst themselves like anxious boys at their father's door, unsure why they have been exiled.

When he emerges, it is to lecture them, his tone weighty and stressed, as if underlining each word. He scolds them for any impulse toward complacency. Our compulsion must always be to see something new, he says.

And in the studio at night, he narrows the aperture, adjusts the focus, and thinks there is something moving in all of this. The way his hands reach around Augustine to rearrange the sheets, their bodies bent together as if embracing. It is as though the two of them are cooperating in some spectacular *trompe l'oeil.*

He presents the photographs as though they are depictions of actual attacks, rather than trances. On the subject of mesmerization, he must remain mute. Meting out his innovative ideas at the tedious pace which his colleagues find palatable. The skeptics offer him no alternative, he tells himself. Frustrated to be confined by the narrowness of other men's minds, by the pettiness of his peers. In the end, they will all benefit from the discoveries that his daring affords. They will label him a visionary. He has no doubt.

I have heard the whispers, he acknowledges, the accusations from certain corners of the medical community that hysteria in its present form seems to exist only in France, only at the Salpêtrière, as if I have fabricated it. It would be a marvelous thing if I could create illnesses according to my whim and fancy. But no one need rely on my word alone. I am nothing more than an intermediary: I transcribe what I see.

He dims the amphitheatre lights, wheeling the camera out in front of the audience, as if it is a being worthy of worship. The room receding in its presence, growing hushed and insubstantial as though objects and audience might suddenly cease to be.

He takes advantage of this opportunity to startle the crowd, pointing the camera in their direction and igniting a blinding flash of magnesium—so that, for an instant, they become the subjects and he and Augustine are left in darkness. Ladies shriek and jump from their seats, dissolving into nervous peals of laughter. Men adjust their monocles and try to stifle their surprise, rubbing their eyes to disperse the afterimage.

He delights in the reaction, savors their discomfort, thrilled at how totally he has them in thrall, like a master of ceremonies who has, at that very moment, perfected his showmanship. He pauses to take it all in. The room once again reduced to silence.

We need only acclimatize the patient to the lens in order to begin our narrative, he tells the spectators. This may require an investment of time, but the results are well worth it.

And he reveals at last his burgeoning *oeuvre,* projecting countless photographs of Augustine's attacks and postures, each more improbable than the last. Documented in black and white, irrefutable. The audience spellbound by the sequences unfurling above their heads.

Ouverture

You allow illustrious visitors in to see the studio—the *atelier vitré*—this chamber that has become our chapel. And their presence seems a sacrilege. The bed an altar upon which I offer myself nightly—to you, *Monsieur*, not to them. They do not belong anywhere within these walls. They are not worthy.

It becomes clear, quickly enough, that your intentions are not to elevate, but to abase. To punish those who have dared to doubt. Entering this hallowed space, even the most prestigious men are pilgrims brought low before you, witnesses passing from daylight into darkness. The curtains drawn hermetically close. The camera displayed like an instrument of inquisition.

Once their eyes have adjusted, you open the curtains, reveal decks built for observation, two-way mirrors, wall upon wall of windows that flood the room with light. Leaving your guests disoriented, exposed. They gaze at you warily, wondering what lesson you intend to bestow, what warning you have issued—that they, too, are under your scrutiny?

Such pettiness seems beneath you, *Monsieur*, like an actor choosing to overplay his part. What if I were to indulge in similar grandstanding, to shift on stage from collaborator to creator, simply to show you that I know how to thrill an audience, command a crowd?

It is not inconceivable, you know. Just, perhaps, unnecessary for now. A slap, when only a nudge is needed.

In the evenings following such intrusions, I refuse to perform, sulking over what you claim is an unintended slight. You tell me, Augustine, breathe deeply, fixing a rag over my face. Your voice low and soothing. Coaxing. Conciliatory. And before my eyes, the fog descends, grey and purled like a shawl, shrouding my vision with its intricate haze, its involutions.

The surge strikes like an electric current, from toes to head, the inferno spreading relentlessly. Augustine, you say, and I remember that there was a saint with that name. As muscle by muscle I push myself toward the sky.

You share nothing of our clandestine encounters, telling the interns it is fatigue that causes you to end your lessons earlier in the evening. When we are alone, you describe the great Christian mystics, women who held the image of their celestial spouse before them as a perpetual vision, a conjugal hallucination. You show me paintings of saints in the throes of convulsions, breasts bared, devils tearing at the bedclothes. You say, this is all religion is, Augustine, this *grande hystérie*—and I peer into the darkness, pledge my troth, and pray for consummation. All these nights with you, and so little air.

In the amphitheatre, you serve me absinthe and opiates until I am no longer certain when I am performing in public and when I'm attending a private bacchanal, a feast at which you are the only guest abstaining. You invite audience members on stage to trigger attacks, their hands reaching and delving to find the hysterogenic points, my entire body sensitized, as if my skin is inside out, each touch directly contacting the nerves. I lunge to kiss their throats, their mouths, wishing they were you. Some men pull away, others press closer, close their eyes, moan, as the interns struggle to separate us, avoiding or seeking out my febrile fingers, my intoxicating hands.

Occasionally, after a performance, an audience member slips backstage. I form a small allegiance of followers, both male and female, patients and practitioners, who court me like suitors—passing me love notes and trinkets, a flower bud smuggled in from the outside, delivered to me bruised and browned, crushed between fabric and breast, but all the more fragrant for its injury.

Instead of growing possessive, you seem to revel in your rivals' weaknesses, to relish the exposure of their desires. You behave like an ascetic, impervious to the appetites of the flesh, retreating behind rigorous self-denial. I parse your words, discover reasons for encouragement, indications that you are not entirely immune to my advances. And I'm not sure which is more tormenting, the existence of hope or its lack. My body arched as if it would break in order to touch you.

As viewers, we must remind ourselves that the patient does not pose to provoke us, you tell the crowd. When confronted with the photographs, that is no easy task. The pictures are saturated with sexuality—so rich they overwhelm, thwart, pervert their captions. Augustine herself is never more feminine than when she is photographed. She flaunts herself before the lens. As self-absorbed as Narcissus, and equally fascinating.

Give her a mirror and she will gaze at herself for hours. And we will linger as well, smitten by the charm of her pose. Who could resist looking a second time, a third, or watching, transfixed, for days, even years? One could spend a lifetime reproducing and repeating this moment, reprovoking the contracture that elicited such an elegant tilt of the head, the cant of that drooping blossom, extending the paralysis that numbed her enough to allow such prolonged contemplation. In this way, the viewer draws a little closer, too close, dangerously close.

⌒

Each night, I invite you into the bed, leave a spot empty beside me, open my arms to you.

I warn you not to keep me waiting. You never know who will respond, *Monsieur*, their presence summoned by your body's absence.

I conjure up rivals, confess to false affairs. I say, *Monsieur,* you do not believe me, and you smile and remain silent. I say, *Maître,* do not doubt me.

Rather than arouse my rage, you confess a secret, tell me you are writing a book about me—a prodigious text, a marvel for the ages. It will be named like a book of the saints, you say. And I whisper, *Augustine*—awed by this idea. But you say no, laughing. No, you say, it will be called *l'Iconographie.* The wondrous word, itself a revelation.

I close my eyes and wait for the spirit to take me, for you to transform before me. I shift from mock crucifixion to masturbation without the slightest reservation. Grabbing your hand and trying to pull you to me. The air thick with an incense of sweat and silver nitrate, ether and smoke.

⌒

The amphitheatre takes on the atmosphere of a bordello. She behaves like an extortionist, determined to reap a bounty from behaviors that are supposed to be involuntary. Her insistence belying her innocence, her lack of conscious control.

She focuses on his face as he watches her, whispers assignations for future rendezvous to whichever intern or audience member stands before her, voice pitched for the stage so that everyone can hear. Each partner blissfully unaware of her intended audience. He, however, has no doubt. Her look is one of desire, directed at him. His visage reflected in the dark discs of her eyes. And under his coat, every muscle tightens.

At first blush, Augustine's self-adornment seems harmless enough, he explains, a conceited flourish that complements her giggling fits and flirtations. But as with any extravagance, what is to constrain the giggle from transforming into mad laughter, what is to rein in the hysteric's compulsion to reimagine herself to the point of falsehood? There is only a fine line between innocence and excess, and the hysteric's impulse will always be to straddle it, legs akimbo, flaunting herself to the point of provocation and scandal.

He puts an abrupt end to the audience's participation, unsure whether he can trust her theatrics, embarrassed by her ardor. Yet even when Augustine is alone on stage, she performs as if accompanied by a partner, her body curved to counterbalance a weight that doesn't exist, a body that doesn't exist. Her postures so evocative that a shadow figure seems to carve itself out of negative space—a palpable presence that she summons to her side.

It is there ever after, this silent and covert companion—an interloper in each and every scene, as if a phantom has been released by his intoxicants, by the sheer force of her stagecraft.

Time after time, he watches her make love to nothing, hands caressing emptiness, pelvis rising and falling in rhythmic thrusts. He sees the flush that creeps over her neck and breast, the rosy patches that resemble fingerprints. And he begins to suspect that her gestures are directed at someone else—an intern, perhaps, or an audience member. Maybe even a fellow patient. Vacillating between the certainty that she is faking her passion and the suspicion that she is reliving an actual incident, an illicit encounter in the wards abetted by his ignorance.

The more he considers it, the more convinced he becomes. And he cannot help but feel a twinge of envy and remorse—a desire to know his rival's name.

M

I SAY, if I tell you this, *Maître*, *Monsieur*, if I tell you this, it is a trust. A *confiance*. Between you and I, *Monsieur*, *vous comprenez?* If I tell you this, of my lover, of M. How can I tell you, *Maître*, where can I begin?

And he carefully notes every effect of the atropine, of the amyl nitrate. And giving her another rag to breathe, he says, tell me Augustine, what do you see.

My beloved M, she starts, I am in bed at night and M enters the room, enters my bed at night. *Maître*, I am so ashamed. And when M comes near, I ask, do you love me, M, do you love me, and M says yes, always yes, and holds me and presses against me. I can feel the palpitations, the hands inside my gown, and when I ask again, I say, do you love me, and it is as if M says no. And I cannot move. Hands on my breasts, palpitations, *Maître*, and chills take me. I do not want you to ignore this. I cannot move my arms. M presses the breath out of me. I cannot breathe. Do not ignore these symptoms, *Maître*, do not, and hands against my thighs, and then, *Monsieur*, *mon professeur*, I feel something that I do not dare describe to you, a sensation that overtakes me stronger than seizure. M does not love me, and yet I am overwhelmed with a happiness that I have not known before, and again when M comes to me like this, ten times a night, *Maître*, ten, and you check on me only twice, and every time that M presses against me, I cannot breathe and cannot talk until I take M into me entirely, and *Maître*, that is all I dare tell you, it is all that I will.

Only this as well, Monsieur Charcot, your intern, entering through the service door, said to me—hello—and asked me, Augustine, what has come over you, because when he grasped my wrist in greeting, like this, *Monsieur*, precisely like this, it was as if a shock were running through me, and it was all I could do to stop from pulling myself to him, he resembled so clearly to me at that moment my darling M, as anyone would I suppose, the woman in the next room, or you yourself, *Maître*, even you, and hands under my nightgown, *Monsieur*, three days of palpitations, *Maître*, three days of this, and shuddering that would not stop for hours.

In my room, I whisper, M, but no one answers, and I wonder if I have angered you—speaking the initial of your name aloud, allowing the elixirs to draw out so many secrets. Your presence penned into his notebook. The way I held you while he watched. But M, it is a bed which he can only see as empty. You gather shadows around you like a sheet, black to my white, a contrast which even the camera does not seem to see.

You arrived like a being conjured from nothingness, from pure desire. Slipping into my embrace in the midst of an attack. Your body molded into the shape of my silhouette, so I knew you first only by the outline that was not my own.

And once I have begun to speak of you, it is as if I cannot stop. I was dreaming again. *Mademoiselle. Madame. Monsieur. Mon cher.* You are a sleek letter. Indescribable. The dark slant of your name. Abridged. It stalks my dreams nightly. M, I was dreaming of you again tonight, *ce soir, mon amante, mon amour.*

I recognize you in everyone—the interns, the doctors, my own face in the mirror. Your features androgynous, discreet, generic enough to belong to anyone, yet undeniably your own. I gather you to me, hold you in the intimacy of this embrace that is not an embrace. Speaking in rhythm metered out in rhyme. *Frissoner.* My enigmatic, my nameless, mine.

Wherever I go, you are. And always it is your name I speak, and always I call you at night. *M'aimes-tu?* You lead me into a landscape I had all but forgotten. That for years I had ceased to envision. Beyond these walls. The promenades and night gardens of the Bois de Boulogne.

But walking through the woods with you, I know we have not made it past the four posts of this bed. You say to me, everything that has occurred inside this room has never in fact occurred. And I know, as always, that what you tell me is true, at the same time that I know this means you too can be unimagined. And I ask you again, *m'aimes-tu?* And always the answer is yes. Until, eventually, it is no. Thigh against my thigh in this drugged bed. Breathless. Your weight so heavy on my chest. The feel of you. It is indescribable, *n'est-ce pas?*

In the Bois de Boulogne, you show me the veins of leaves and tear around them until they emerge skeletal. Placing one first on the back of my hand and then on my palm like a glorious map. You reveal an entire realm of yellow-toed salamanders living under rocks, butterflies lurking in the underbrush, insects working their way into the trunks of the trees. The mushrooms placed on my tongue taste like the dark smoky space between one's legs. My hand in the dirt. And nothing has ever felt this soft before.

You will always remain out of focus. My M. Safe pseudonym. They have nothing to name you. They never will.

∾

When you retire to your study, *Maître*, M enters the studio surreptitiously, loosening the restraints, rubbing the redness from my skin. Together, we experiment with new positions. M stretches my legs, massaging the muscles to keep them limber, working the joints to improve flexibility and balance. Our bodies creating unorthodox compositions.

And I imagine the lens is a peephole delivering images directly to your eye.

M plays doctor, lover, partner, priest, and I play along, allow my imagination to take hold. We weave elaborate dramas, perform plots stolen from novels and dreams. Feeding off each other, striving to surpass our improvisations, to flesh out our roles.

I reenact my infidelities on stage, *Monsieur*, perform as the neglected wife, the willing adulteress. Sometimes I reverse chronology —begin with the climax of an encounter and work my way backward to the courtship, an inversion that allows me to maintain the virgin's blush no matter how provocative my behavior.

Sometimes I play the courtesan, addressing you brazenly before the audience. Do not worry, *Maître*, I assure you, there is room for three in the enormity of our *boudoir*.

And yet I must admit, you suffer some diminishment. The space I need you to fill is smaller now.

In the studio at night, I observe the arthritic motions of your hands. Your knuckles cracking as you unfurl your fingers. They swing like pendulums from the edges of your palms, as if each one, at any moment, could free itself from the knotted network of your hands. Who would have thought you were so old, *Maître*. Who would have believed you were of the body at all, or that in you, there could be anything resembling age.

Focus, Augustine, you say to me again and again. Focus.

And raising a magnet above my breast, you pass it over the cavity of my sternum to the other side, watching eagerly. From your eyes, I feel the pull begin, the transfer of pain from place to place, the intent focus like a clamp upon the breast. Your gaze fixed. Where you hold the magnet above me, I contract my muscles, and you say, Augustine, amazing, amazing. And in an instant you are young again, a boy watching sleight of hand, ardently impressed as you move the metal from spot to spot, and I, *Maître*, move in every way imaginable.

You spend hours calling forth the flowers of every terrain, birds, beasts, even lovers—my Mesmer, my *Maître*, my madman magician—trying to coax me to reveal a name. But I have none to offer you, only an initial. Seductive in its simplicity. Dearest M, *ma chérie, mon cher.*

I say, *Maître*, it is a trust you cannot, will not, keep. And you bring out the morphine, the *nitrate d'amyle*. You wait until I am on good behavior every time. And then you say, Augustine. Augustine, you say, *écris tout*.

I react to your frustration with barely suppressed delight, relishing this rivalry, the evidence of an attachment beyond indifference. I do everything I can to enflame your ardor, to pique your jealousy.

On stage, I blow a kiss to M, but you assume it is meant for you, a flush settling into the wrinkles of your cheeks, spreading to your collar.

M urges me to be cautious, tells me envy is a vengeful master. Worried that you will punish me for my indiscretions. I swear to be more discreet—doing so more as an act of appeasement than out of any real apprehension.

I see no reason why I could not have you both.

And I say mmm. And I say M. And I say, always it is my beloved M of whom I dream. *Monsieur. Madame. Maître. Moi-même.* And surely this at least is true.

Sécrétions

IN THE STUDIO AT NIGHT, he is filled with the fervor of an interrogator seeking definitive fact, concocting combinations of narcotics that he administers as truth serums to determine if her lover exists. Yet her confessions do nothing to assuage his uncertainty. Every admission offset by a denial. He must resort to asking the same questions as any common cuckold—demanding a name, an explanation—disturbed by her effortless ability to prevaricate.

In her extreme isolation, the hysteric will seek out companionship, he tells the audience sternly, watching the faces around him for a flicker of guilt or smirk of satisfaction.

If she cannot find a companion, she invents one. She appeals to her lover repeatedly—with pleas, kisses, open arms. Her body poised in anticipation of an ever-imminent arrival.

Those of us who diagnose her know we must avoid the temptation to cast ourselves as the romantic lead, alone on the stage as we are with her. Yet we cannot help but imagine ourselves filling that embrace, occupying that emptiness. Such is the power of the aptly named *attitudes passionelles*—poses agitated, furtive, and fulminating all at once, in their desperate visibility. They seem to demand a narrative, a telling of delirious liaisons.

He scans the crowd again, feeling suddenly exposed, foolish. His cheeks reddening.

Of course, the hysteric's encounters are with absence, he continues. In a way, these incidents are the epitome of innocence—as intercourse is wholly denied—yet the hysteric's behavior renders that description perverse. She compels our gaze to the point of exhaustion, insisting we observe acts of near pornographic proportion, complete with pseudo-climaxes and gratuitous spasms. We must remember: each orgasm is dry, diffracted, a mere simulacrum of intimacy.

Such couplings are frequently produced but never reproductive, he says, except in the images we create of them.

In photographs, M appears as a shadow, obscured and out of focus. An indistinct figure caught on the edge of the composition, in the process of fleeing the shot. A presence as distracting and abrasive as a mote of dust trapped in the lashes. The shape could easily be a defect in processing, an irregularity created when the plates are dried above spirit lamps or when wet collodion is applied. But he cannot shake the notion that it is a person who accidentally lingered too long in the periphery of the lens, captured in the aftermath of infidelity.

He relies on the camera's ability to act as both spy and warden, trusts its unflinching gaze to apprehend the truth. Photography is an honest art, he warns the audience, the interns. It is incontestably faithful. The print reveals the slightest of flaws, alongside the most flagrant indiscretions. That is why the apparatus has found such efficacious use as an instrument of surveillance and identification.

One day, this tool may give us the foresight to recognize criminality, venality, even madness, in a person who has yet to commit her first sin. Until that day, we build a case against the hysteric, one photograph at a time—each frame offering evidence to strengthen our scientific conviction. We force her to reveal the most damning of secrets, until she has nothing left to expose.

After a single application of ether, she sways her hips, experiences climaxes on the spot, tempting him repeatedly to verify their physical authenticity. Afraid that his pronouncements are in fact incorrect. It is a matter that keeps him awake at night, debating whether he should cross that audacious threshold, discover once and for all if her pleasure is genuine.

He dreams of women soaking in electrostatic baths, their knees draped over the rims of steel receptacles, their vulvas blooming like a field of fetid roses. *Les fleurs du mal, les flueurs blanches.* The women lie with their heads barely above water level—sirens submerged. Each tub an ocean. Each body aquatic, effluvial, as he scrapes and exsiccates uterine walls. Basins filling with the brackish runoff, condensation running in rivulets down bathhouse tiles. The women have simmered for months, bodies softening until the membranous parts, like parchment, have dissolved, detached—exiting through the bladder, excreted through the pores. He uses a system of weights and pulleys to winch each woman from the water, dredging the defluent bodies from their immersions so he can complete brief inspections, testing the suppleness of the women's skin, prying back the peeling layers. He parts their thighs, searching for something solid, some internal substance that will not deliquesce. The women suspended, ponderous and dripping, as he nestles between their knees, bowed before that wet shrine. He lowers them back into the water, applies the current, and watches as their lithe bodies wriggle and flop— careful not to touch the water lest he himself be shocked.

We cannot allow ourselves to be faint of heart when faced with even the most intimate verifications, he tells the audience. I am speaking of collecting the secretions of the body. In every form. Tears, sweat, saliva, blood, urine, even vaginal discharge. The hysterics' abundance must be used to our advantage. We must not only condone it, but compel it, push to the limit their penchant for oozing, their propensity to seep. We must create a compendium of ejaculations, note variations in color, temperature, texture, odor.

The men in the audience draw deep breaths, as the women raise smelling salts to their noses. This is a protocol that must be pursued, he insists. Briquet went so far as to manually stimulate his hysterics, to prescribe a regimen of copulation that ended only when the body was utterly drained. We have other means at our disposal. We can use Augustine's encounters with her lover to our advantage, uncover the extent to which she exaggerates in order to arouse jealousy, to induce passion.

Consider for a moment: what would physicians do if bodies themselves began to lie? How could medicine be practiced honestly? When dealing with frauds and cheats, it is the body that betrays the mendacity, that bares the truth with its tells and flushes. We depend on it to do so.

His experimental detour draws the disapproval of the orthodoxy, along with accusations of perversion, decrees demanding that the pious stay away. Their exodus comes almost as a relief to him—their seats filled soon enough by atheists and intellectuals, scientists and sophisticates.

I am not a miracle worker, he insists to the audience, I am an artist. And as an artist, I retain the right to be infernal, to pursue chaos to her dark and dank abyss.

Despite the boldness of his words, he cannot easily bring himself to act. The bed, a stage from which even he is excluded.

Repeatedly, she clasps her hands together, watching the air above her for deliverance. But he cannot tell whom she is beseeching, whom she is rebuffing. The longer he watches her, the greater his doubt becomes. Her attention wholly absorbed, so that it feels as if he is not even standing on the stage beside her.

In the studio at night, he says, Augustine, and she does not respond to him—reacts instead by turning away, summoning M into her bed.

Having grown accustomed to her desire, he resents her distraction. His hand hesitating on her pelvis, so close to her groin, until finally he can no longer deny his need to know. Shocked to discover that after each encounter with M, she moistens and exudes, a fact that seems to disprove the fictiveness of her lover, that disputes some of his most vehement assertions. His fingers delicately probing the recesses of her sex.

And he wonders what else she is concealing, what lies he has mistaken as truths.

Enquête

THE BODY THAT EXUDES SECRETES THE SECRETS OF ITS ILLNESS, he tells the interns, with a slight tone of accusation. Our task is to decipher the meaning—decode the messages conveyed in spittle and foam, lachrymas and micturitions. They are like letters left at the bedside, *les billets doux,* incriminating traces excreted as evidence.

The question confronting us is this: can we ever drain our patient of her potential to deceive? Can we protect the most naïve among us from succumbing to her charms? *Messieurs, mes élèves,* never underestimate the craft, sagacity, and perseverance which women, under the influence of this great disease, will put into play for the purposes of misdirection—especially when the physician is to be the victim.

We have machines for extracting confessions and exposing untruths, inventions still in their infancy that must be nurtured and explored, even when their use seems unnecessary. Take, for example, the field of faradization. Baraduc experimented extensively with currents and conduction. Hysteria, he concluded, was an illness of contact. A truth to which perhaps only Augustine can attest.

In the laboratory, he wires women like lamps. And she finds herself standing before him, threaded with cord and scorched by electrical impulse. In these moments, her mind is nothing more than a blank-ness, a blur, but in the minutes before and between, she wonders what clarity he is trying to produce. Her brain suddenly illuminated.

She thinks that if she could, she would render herself all light for him, in order to stop this constant series of shocks. The numb-ing electricity that spreads from the center out to every nerve. She would become lucid. Luminous. She would be enough to see by. And Augustine, he would say, Augustine. Stunned out of words.

He aspires to an industry of standardization, verification. He says, everything, *mesdames et messieurs*—I assure you—everything is quan-tifiable. And numbers do not lie.

Here, you see we have blanketed Augustine in labels and probes, smothered her with sensors—myographs, pneumographs—in order to measure her jolts and convulsions, to track her special sensibili-ties. I see no advantage to testing on animals. I cannot justify taking poor, dumb creatures and subjecting them to the whims of science, all to confirm certain postulations about the human nervous system. My peers and predecessors, unfortunately, disagree. We know that Magnan delighted in instigating hallucinations and seizures in dogs, injecting them with absinthe. Claude Bernard sedated rabbits with chloroform before applying electric current to their facial muscles. I prefer to go directly to the source, to fellow humans who have sought out my help, subjected themselves willingly to my ministrations. Any other path, to me, seems immoral.

I say, *Maître,* what exactly do you think is wrong? Gasping for air. Unable to breathe. You chart every respiration, marking it with a dot, connecting each point with a continuous line. The precipitous rises. The profound drops. It is like watching my death plotted. These signs which signal suffocation. This terrible lack of air. I ask myself how far you will allow this to go. My body broken down into strange sets of numbers until I barely recognize myself. Everything measured—the time it takes me to raise my arm, the angle of my eye, the number of steps until I find myself at your side.

You keep careful watch on the chronometer, ticking out the timing of every attack. You write—18 seconds of menace, 10 seconds of appeal, 14 of lewdness, 24 of ecstasy, 22 in which rats are seen, 17 in which music is heard, 13 seconds of snapping in time with the shutter of the camera, followed by 23 seconds of lamentation. You put the numbers together like equations—trying to find my absolute value, my root, the multiple by which your theorems may be proven. And I wonder whether I am merely an inequality to you, a problem to be solved.

You say, the hysteric takes pleasure in distorting, in making her symptoms extraordinary, in making herself. And I grow indignant at the accusation. What have I possibly done to displease you? What emotion I have not offered you at night, in bed, vapors of ether settling around me?

Monsieur, I admonish, there is no need for electricity, simply ask and my body will provide. As you charge the pincers for another round, and I brace for the impending surge.

You tell me M is just an illusion born of illness, but your inflection turns the assertion into question. You demand evidence of our encounters, ask for proof that I cannot provide.

I tell you everything, and you, in turn, repeat it to the audience—though never accurately. Speaking of M as a fiction I have invented. The easy way in which you make everything sound untrue. By the time I think to assuage your jealousy, it is too late. Each session an interrogation in which my body bears witness against itself, time and time again.

This space offers nothing to hold onto, the laws of attraction and repulsion hopelessly distorted. My body irresistible one moment, repellant the next.

When I reach for you, my arms bend backward, my body pressing upward, pressing away, despite my effort to draw you to me, to allay your suspicions.

Maître, I say. And my voice moves you farther from my side.

You say, the patient's pain begins at the nerve trunk and localizes in the joints or muscle before spreading throughout the limb. Any pressure causes the skin to redden, the temperature of the affected area rising rapidly. More often than not, this will result in hemiplegia—a numbness that extends along the right side of her body, affecting the mucous membranes, auditory canal, eyelid, eye, tongue, palate, vulva.

You point to my crimson and fevered leg and I can sense the feeling slipping away, drawn out by the gesture of your hand, the severity of your voice.

It is as if I am divided into quadrants, hemispheres. You, the jealous despot, commandeering entire regions at will. The lack of sensation spreading until half my body has disappeared. I say, tell me, *Maître,* what is to the right of me, in the spaces I cannot see? My garbled speech a slur of broken letters, missing vowels.

M tries to restore sensation, rubbing my right leg, holding my limp hand, prying open my drooping eyelid. But still, I feel nothing. Trapped in a body more yours than my own.

You pass elongated needles through my anaesthetized arm to prove how completely feeling has been lost—in through the center and out the other side. You work steadily, as if I am a doll you are creating stitch by stitch, a poppet or some witch's toy. The needle breaks the surface of skin, leaving pinholes and points of blood behind.

Surely, if any sensation remained, you insist, she would react to our punctures and penetrations.

My body barbed, stuck full of pins and needles. A hexing doll whose own limbs are afflicted. A curse turned inward.

During such spells, you tell the audience, Augustine tries to teach herself to be left-handed. And you produce roll after roll of paper, covered in writing's unraveled threads.

Hysterics try to communicate at any cost, and yet their histories, their stories, matter little to us in terms of the disease. Their professions of love, their avowals of honesty are meaningless. Though we recognize the patient's language, we must nonetheless ignore her words.

You glance down at me skeptically, as if everything about me is mere figment and falsehood, and I know that you have said this precisely to hurt me. To show me my place in this equation—as a void, perhaps, an emptiness.

For the first time before the crowd, you reach inside me, your arm plunging impossibly deep, as if you would force your entire body within—shoulders head waist feet—an old man intent on rebirth.

You split me apart, *Monsieur*, pause only when you find the uterus, the pulse of it convulsive, like my body on the table. And in one unstoppable movement, you grab hold, squeezing the organ until I freeze in place. Motionless. Throbbing. The audience staring at us like we are an aberration of nature—joined, as we are, in the most intimate of places.

You maintain this position for only an instant. Moving quickly to withdraw your hand, to relieve the audience's evident discomfort.

The excruciating pain of birthing as your arm emerges and the seizures begin again.

The eyes of the audience intolerable in this moment. My dress pulled up.

The horror of this, something I will experience for hours.

In the studio at night, I whisper, *Maître, mon dieu, mon diable.* Your gaze inquisitive, cruel, as if tinged by something infernal. You respond slowly, pondering my words with the solemnity of a man weighing his soul on the scales. If I was the Good Lord, Augustine, you say, I would have neither beginning nor end, and that would ultimately bore me: once everything was made, what would I do then? You fall silent, sunk in contemplation, until an idea inspires you and then you smile like a devil with his plan. Your words expelled with a hiss: I would amuse myself by undoing, perhaps.

You count my life away, one movement at a time. The unbearable acts of addition. The parts of me that are slowly but surely subtracted. I think of all the hours I have given you. Divided down to their very seconds. And I realize it is all an exercise, isn't it? Some sort of staggering experiment, on knees, on back, always in some subtle state of stupefaction. Each time I enter the amphitheatre and reach for you, *Maître,* I find the ramp instead—leading me to the stage, leading me on, to this show-all event. Your body just another curtain, another screen behind which the audience awaits.

I have told you all that you have asked of me and more. I have given you my words without knowing who you will give them to. And, in turn, you have made me a wanton woman, defamed in public, the object of a peepshow. Men pressing their eyes to glass, watching everything I do.

And it is chilling. Your knowledge of clamps and braces, of currents run through the base of the brain, of needlework that will not sever any major veins.

I am your curiosity. And your curiosity, *Maître*, is boundless.

III.

Sommeil
1880

SHE FALLS INTO A DORMANCY THAT LASTS FOR DAYS. Face flushed, limbs fixed in attitudes of repose that cannot be easily altered— a relaxation that is in fact rigidity, her eyes moving beneath the lids as if absorbed in dream. But there is nothing restful about it. This suspension that is like a waking somnambulism. This semblance of sleep. Low breath. Dreams she does not know to be dreams.

He claims that he can wake her with an ovarian compression, but he does not try. Wheeling her into the amphitheatre instead, telling the audience that she has slept for seven days without ceasing. And he shows them how nothing, not the noise of a drum, the inhalation of ammonia, or the electrical stimulation of the skin, muscles, nerve stems will awaken her. He increases the voltage—her reveries electrified as she is shocked into stranger and stranger states of slumber.

Torpor taking over. The languor of limbs.

In the studio at night, which for her might as well be day, he studies her parted lips, her shallow breaths, trying to distinguish if she is dreaming of him. He tells his audience tales of somnolent women found in woods, but catching himself, says, of course these are only stories, embellished by art, of a young hysteric discovered by a youth-ful and scatterbrained prince.

The bed against her back. The trees arched above her head.

He focuses on her face for hours. The shutter opening and closing in place of her eyelids, which remain unnaturally still. After the first few frames, he finds he cannot take another picture. It feels like sac-rilege in the hush of that room—the camera clicking like an intruder between them. Shutting the door, he hoods the lens and regards her without the aid of that third eye. With only his own.

There is a tightness around her ribs, as if embracing, and she utters, M, and M is not with her—off in a forest that she can only guess is around her. Embowered.

She whispers, *Maître,* but he too is missing. Her eyelids stuck to-gether as if they have been stitched shut. She is only able to lift them for seconds at a time. Images revealed to her in glimpses—her arms crossing her breasts, holding herself.

Sometimes when she opens her eyes, she finds herself clasped by the arms of strangers, odd metal forearms, or the dark claws of beasts. Sometimes there are women weeping over her.

In the branches, a woman marked like a witch.

Every time he enters the room, to reencounter her, he is astounded again by her beauty. His *dormeuse.* He cherishes this time, when he can watch unseen, unobserved, even by her—believing it is his choice to wake her or leave her wandering in the wildwood. Day after day. Night after night.

She dreams of strangers in the Bois de Boulogne. One after another touching her lips, her thighs, her neck. M comes to her and tells her dreams, and she asks, is that what I am doing? But M does not reply.

The strangers pry apart her legs to look at her reveries, which fall from her like photographs, stilled and weighty things. *Le Maître* catching them in his hands and turning them into projections flashed against the wall of the wood. He pushes one hand and then the other inside her to reach the most reluctant of *rêves—les cauchemars*. The negative plates splintering glass, emerging with organs trailing bloody behind them.

Days pass without demarcation. In the studio, her face is unguarded, her body given over to him entirely, but at the same time, it is not— her expression enigmatic, her skin like a screen he cannot see past. At times he imagines that she is dreaming them all out of existence, like the princess who sent courtiers and castle into a slumber that ended only when she awoke. Afraid he has become merely a fragment of her dreams.

Her eyes moving back and forth too quick to measure. The oracular globes convulsing. Respiration thready and irregular.

He tells the audience, insistently, that this is just a transformation of the classic convulsive attack, that such phenomena have occurred throughout history. But the word *transformation* unsettles him, makes him think of women turned into trees, or men made stags and torn apart by their own dogs—transmutations, metamorphoses. As if the body would turn itself inside out, reveal some monster hidden within, or the plush insides of skin and vein.

Her cycles align themselves to a new set of seasons—rapid, tumultuous, unpredictable. When she menstruates, the woods are lashed with rain and crimson foliage spills from her sex. The wind, rushing through the branches, causes the trees to hum like tuning forks—trunks fastened with clamps to prevent them from falling. Strangers cowering under a canopy of boughs. Saplings bowed to the ground.

Veins branch visibly against her thinning skin, bones push their way to the surface. Sixteen days and counting. Her hair grows knotted and root-wild. The bedsheets beneath her, stiff with urine, are changed every other day. The interns forcing water between her clenched jaws, applying ointment to the raised red welts, the splits and scratches where her skin has broken down.

Hysterical somnolence is a form of play-acting in which the body colludes, he says, staging scenarios for the audience. Imagine a child playing Beauty in the Woods who falls asleep doing so—her act of imagination, which is absorbed by the body, causes an actual physiological event to occur. Perhaps it will be a kiss that rouses her, but perhaps it will be a call to supper instead.

Here, we have less choice in awakening—the hysterical body being infamously obstinate—but nevertheless we are aware of the act. We can appreciate it for what it truly is—stagecraft.

But looking down at her lips, which are cracked and bloody from days of dryness, he wonders whether he can in fact wake her.

It frightens her, how long he is willing to linger, the smell of him above her like the underside of fallen leaves. It is as if he has no other task, no duties he must fulfill—he simply waits and watches her sleep. Sometimes lifting and prodding her in order to get a better view, or repositioning her stiffened limbs to feign some semblance of life. He props her against tree trunks and says her name slowly, but it tumbles out and drops like stone before it ever reaches her ears. His hand pushing inside her to pull forth the plates that have developed—a sequence of images that he reads like auguries, searching for something that will tell him what to do. His fingers cold inside her. Expectant.

And she asks, M, am I dreaming? And M says, shh, the spectators are still filling the seats. She sighs and says, *ça, c'est toujours le même.* And she asks, M, do you love me? But all she can hear is hundreds of feet trampling the forest floor.

∾

An attack of torpitude is an attack stopped, he explains, or slowed down past the point of visible observation. It may very well be that the patient is experiencing the manifestation of symptoms so intermittently and on such a gradual scale that we do not see them occurring.

He tries to imagine instruments sensitive enough to measure and mark her repose, to reveal what he can no longer observe behind her lids. The eyeballs roving aimlessly when he pries them open—glazed and unaware, as if following a watch swung before them. Hypnotized before he can even lift an object in front of her and say, Augustine, tell me, what do you see.

The woods are illuminated by lightning flashes, an electrical crack splintering the trees around her into needle-thin slivers, broken branches sharp like brambles. In the distance, the sound of an ax striking bark repeatedly. When she opens her eyes, the leaves are cloth patterns cut and stitched to the stems of the trees, filtering light upon her as she drowses in the clearing, defenseless. The storm converging above her, drawing moisture from her body, static sparking at her scalp like a galvanized crown.

And nightly, now, he is struck by bouts of insomnia, waking reveries, until it seems that her sleep, like a lodestone, has reversed the poles around which they circle.

∞

Her skin grows pale, sleep draining the color from her cheeks—he imagines—into her dreams. And when he enters the room now, it is as if he is confronting a statue—her attack frozen and marbleized before him, a shrine to a goddess he is not supposed to see.

He says, she sleeps, if it can be called sleep, and there is good reason to suppose that she will not awaken anytime soon. As each day, the audience grows increasingly restless, waiting for reassurance which he pretends to provide. The skin under his eyes black as bruises. One waits, he says, without anxiety—knowing as we do, with conviction, that one beautiful day, sooner or later, it will all spontaneously stop, without a single kiss required. And the audience laughs. And *le Maître* laughs. Uneasily.

He tells her stories. Lullabies. Unsure if it is to modulate her slumber or assure his own. Wincing with each word spoken, as if only his voice sustains the reality in which the room exists, stationary and knowable. As if without the anchor of his words the entire asylum would evaporate. At times, it seems that her dreams have dissolved matter itself and that his tongue is stitching it back together, words spilling from his mouth like a thick skein of cloth. He picks at the edges of her slumber, trying desperately to make it unravel.

Passing a needle through the center of her hand, he says, Augustine, awake. And he waits for her limbs to move as they often have, in sleep as well as seizure. Before this stillness set in—deeper than any inhalation.

She thinks, there is a room in a tower and a spindle in the studio, spectators sitting in seats made of moss, there are strangers. And the shock of lightning sent through the brain. All she needs is to remove the sliver of wood which has worked its way into her palm and she will awaken. She does not know how she knows this, but she does. Knows too that everything depends upon who wakens her. She pinches the splinter tightly between her fingers and in the forest around her, the dreams fall like leaves.

Réveil

I AWAKE TO THE FLASH OF A PHOTOGRAPH and a world turned black and white. I am grey. Grey teeth. Grey hair sprouting from my head, from my groin, from the darker hollows of my armpits. Protruding around my aureoles like silvered needles. The room bereft of color, as if everything inside is made of iron and merely masking itself as wood, linen, molding, flesh.

I scan my surroundings for some hint of context. Desperate to determine how much time has passed—how many days, decades, centuries. Afraid I have slept my life away behind these walls. Leaving behind what legacy, what mark of myself?

I do not know if it is with relief or regret that I realize how little has changed. The depletion of shade and tone the only difference. A fade to monochrome that deprives every space of depth, dimension. As if the asylum has been reduced to a representation of itself, trapping me inside a flattened frame. Corridors constricted like veins on the verge of collapsing, columns bleached and ossified.

If this is a nightmare, I have not woken yet. Chloroform in the air. The noise of the camera. Its ceaseless clicking.

No matter how much I blink, rub my eyes, the world remains ashen and fixed, achromatic. I arch upward and wonder if the sky still exists above the heavy buttressed ceilings.

Is there anything more than this, I ask M, motioning to the backdrop, to the array of props. I shake my head in disbelief. *Vraiment, c'est tout?*

M indicates beyond the shuttered windows, describes cities and boulevards, canals and *arrondissements*, a landscape too variegated for me to imagine. And I struggle to get my bearings.

∞

In the studio at night, you show me the newest camera, unveiling it before me like a portrait you are presenting. And truly, *Maître,* it is amazing. Its burnished body and multiple *objectifs*—row upon row of lenses meant to capture my movements frame by frame.

You tell me it is pure inspiration. Divine, Augustine, you say— it is divine—a being born of myth, its conception seeded by my slumber. Emerging from your mind like a tri-leveled beast.

And as you prepare the many-eyed monster, fussing over it like a new father, you recite the story of its genesis. It is the tale of Hera, you say, who in her jealousy approached ever-watchful Argus. There were eyes spread all over his body, you whisper, hundreds. He only ever closed two to drowse.

I shudder. Your voice hushed like a nursemaid spreading nightmares.

Hera asked him to watch her husband's lover, who nonetheless escaped, you say. I think of M and ask, but *Maître,* how could she move beneath so many eyes? Your answer, slow and deliberate, building the anxiety, increasing the suspense: because one by one they were lulled to sleep.

Your hand on the shutter. Your eyes upon mine.

The first flash is all but obliterating, the beams entering my eyes, my mouth, my ears, the dark region of my sex—they fill me, strike me rigid, the light so bright that it becomes incarnate, palpating inside me. Each nerve vivified, engorged. I throw my arms out wide, crucified by the radiance, incandescence bleeding in droplets from my forehead and hands, from my ankles, transforming me into a holy spirit, a lucid body. Bursting from my mouth, from my nipples, in rays brilliant to behold.

Without light, you tell the audience, the body could produce no image, leaving us no medium with which to work, only corruptible and transient tissue. But light and flesh—theirs is a fruitful union. Light penetrates, impregnating the body like the Greek gods who raped mortal women, dazing them with resplendence.

Watch how readily the hysteric absorbs this illumination. For a moment, she brims with a blazing visibility, but it is gone in an instant, transferred to the photographic plate, begetting the portrait. Ultimately, like any divinity, the offspring outstrips its mortal mother, imbued with an immortality she can never attain.

We, ladies and gentlemen, become guardians of this scion, this demigod.

We coax from the patient even the most embryonic image, which she offers us willingly, more often than not. If she refuses, we snatch it from her by force—like an infant from its mother's arms—before she thinks the better of it.

The apparatus draws more and more of me into itself. It is like one of your magnets, *Monsieur*, the irresistible pull, the power. I wonder where the images go. They must be so much smaller than me, and thin like skin cut by a scalpel. Hundreds of Augustines trapped within, stacked one atop the other. The only progeny I will ever produce.

Once I have conceived of them, I cannot stop picturing their pale faces, their waiflike bodies nestled in darkness. I ask M, are they beautiful? *Mes petites filles?*

But M has not seen them, is not sure that they even exist. This notion has never occurred to me. After all, what corroboration do I have? What evidence? Perhaps it is all a perverse game—the box empty, the plates blank. Perhaps I pose for nothing, your gestures behind the lens elaborate pantomimes, jokes made at my expense. I have no way of knowing. No remedy except belief.

I beg you to show them to me, these pictures you claim to have made of me. Portraits painted by a box. I say, proof, *Maître*, I need proof. But the curtain remains closed as images are birthed and adjusted, everything carefully prepared behind the vitreous lid of studio glass. Your eyeball pressed to monocle pressed to lens pressed to flesh, evoking the error that an ear must be near, ready to listen, willing to hear.

I say, show me my picture, a photograph of me, please. In place of your answer, the camera responds, clucking like a tongue in dour disapproval.

M coos to me, comforts me, tries to assure me that in time all will be revealed, stroking my stomach, touching my thighs. But I keep my eye on the apparatus, its belly bulging with images it will not deliver to anyone but you, depositing them discreetly into your awaiting hands.

One night, I catch you in a tale-telling mood. Calibrating my words carefully so as not to dispel the inclination, I ask, *Maître*, who lulled the monster to sleep, who convinced Argus to close his eyes? You say, it was Mercury, the patron god of vagabonds and rogues, travelers and thieves. He told Argus fictions, soothed him with stories, songs, the sounds of a flute.

And what happened to Argus, I ask—after he fell asleep? After his head dropped to his breast, exposing his neck? After every lid closed?

Mercury cut off his head, you reply curtly, and the girl escaped.

And his eyes? I ask. You sigh, settling in for the duration.

Hera couldn't bear to see them dimmed so suddenly, you explain. Instead, she scooped them from their sockets, clearing away the viscera. She gathered the orbs in the folds of her skirt, like berries from the field, and carried them carefully to her home on Mount Olympus. In her gardens roamed the most beautiful bird, a peacock, the first of its kind, and she fastened the eyes to its tail feathers, where they remain.

And Mercury, *Maître?* What story did he tell to Argus, I ask, to make him fall asleep?

He told him of Syrinx, you respond, the beautiful huntress. A chaste, virgin nymph—chased by satyrs, pursued by lustful Pan. The horned god caught her on the banks of a river, but she cried out to her sister-nymphs for aid. They instantly transformed her so that, as his arms embraced her, Pan found himself holding nothing but a tuft of reeds, all that was left of the nymph's body. He sighed in despair, and his breath on the reeds produced a plaintive melody that charmed the goat-legged god. He cut the reeds, bound them with wax, and formed them into a flute, a pan flute, which he named syrinx, after the virgin who—from that day forward—he held freely in his hands, pressed to his lips, caressed with his hairy fingers. Each touch producing the most beautiful sounds—melodies fit to murder a monster.

Behind the lens, veiled, blackened, your body merges with those of beasts. Nocturnal. Predatory. The hunched nightmare perched on the end of my bed.

I try to hold the photographs within me, my abdomen swelling with the effort. I keep my legs crossed at all times. Will not allow your speculum inside.

Our extractions—our interventions—are truly acts of mercy, for anything remaining in the hysteric's custody would most certainly be destroyed, you say. We must remember, *messieurs et mesdames,* that the hysteric is a woman in perpetual mourning. Every life she draws to her ends up dead in her arms. It is a true tragedy. In her loneliness, the hysteric reaches out—Bacchic, raving—wishing for nothing more than to find communion, companionship, some connection outside of herself. Instead, her every action engenders annihilation. Like Agave, she returns to consciousness to find her son's head bloody in her arms, his body scattered and torn. And she, more alone than ever, stripped of hallucinatory delusions, must recognize the mangled flesh she holds in her hands. Thus, any moment of lucidity, any return to her senses, is ultimately unbearable.

In my dreams, I convulse under the camera's myriad eyes. Black pupils on white bedsheets, all focused on the birthing bed. My contractions irregular. The apparatus bearing down, aperture fully dilated. You extract the photographs with metal pincers, deliver breech births that make me tear and bleed. Each infant unseen, untouched— offspring aborted. A lens pressed to my breast. *L'objectif. L'objet.*

Milk leaks from my nipples, curdling into silver nitrate, collodion. Pooling in my empty arms. The rats gnaw the placenta, devour the gristly umbilical cord, until all evidence of afterbirth is gone.

When I awake, M cannot console me. I am inconsolable.

There are days when the slightest light burns through pupil and retina, when I refuse to open my eyes, to provoke this pain. But you, *Maître*, so intent on capturing your shot, tell me tales of photophobics unwilling to sit before the lens, to open their eyes. Their resistance conquered by a simple procedure—a slice through the suborbital nerves. You say this wide-eyed, unblinking. I focus again on the camera, on the phosphorous flash. You coo to me like I am a bird to be calmed, as you scour my pupils with blazing filaments, and I step back, flinching, sightless for days.

We expect optical attacks, you tell the audience, the only unpredict-ability is what form the distortion will take. For Augustine, it is a reduction rather than a radiance: the world blanched and blackened.

Some hysterics lose every ideation of form and color, lose their ability to imagine—unable to recognize their relatives, themselves. Faces forgotten. They dream without images, victim to a sort of visual amnesia, making medicine a science of unrecollected dreams, intimately imagined.

I watch the interns scribbling down your words—white pages reflecting back featureless faces. They raise their gaze to me briefly: a wall of black eyes opening, closing, opening, as they blink me into focus and out again.

The first time you show me my photograph, I do not understand—terrified to touch it, to touch myself. It is as if I have left behind my shadow or stepped out of my skin unwittingly, laying it aside on a thin plate of glass only to find myself trapped outside of it, like a mirror that usurps one's likeness. I sit for hours in perfect immobility, mimicking the figure before me, thinking that, perhaps, if I remain composed, it will return to me. Restored to motion only when you order me dragged from the room. Screaming, clawing after what the camera has spirited or conjured away—this self the lens has distilled. That, once taken, doubles, triples itself, multiplying until I am surrounded by faces that both are and are not my own. And I cannot tell if they are doubles of me or I of them—fixed and rigid as we are.

The next morning, sheets pressed between my legs cannot staunch the bleeding.

I invoke Mercury, maenads, M—demand retribution for the machine's sacrilege, the monster's heresy. This sterilization that requires no surgery, only the unceasing slice of the shutter. This radical abortion. But my appeals go unanswered. The apparatus staring me down.

I try not to face it directly, uncertain of what it might steal. Each lens an eye searching for entry. The shutters flutter like lashes, opening and closing in a series of winks, glances, blinks. And I imagine poses so prolonged that their stillness would subdue the camera, seizures so violent that lens after lens would shatter.

You have left me a barren woman, *Maître,* one who produces only redundancy, stillbirths with glazed eyes, livid faces. Teeth bared.

I ooze for days, staining bedsheets and nightgowns. The interns collect and measure the blood, express concern as to when it will end.

When they summon you, you arrive at my bedside empty-handed, smug, insisting that there was no miscarriage, only a misunderstanding, a misconception—that the photographs issue forth not

from the body, but from the chemical bath. Laughing at my confu-
sion, at the way I cover my bloated belly with both hands.

Here, you say, see for yourself. You usher me past the studio, the low-
lit corridor taking several circuitous turns before ending at a doorway
draped in heavy cloth—the entrance to the darkroom. Ready yourself, you whisper, sweeping aside the thick brocade curtain, leaving
my eyes no time to adjust.

We step inside a room steeped in darkness. I squint until, slowly,
the color red returns, creeping in at the edges, spreading over the
walls, the tables, the narrow aisles between. The room stained with
remnants of afterbirth, ruptured placental veins.

You lead me to a vat of liquid, foul-smelling but clear, not brackish
or bloody. A reflecting pond over which I hover, extraneous, uncertain
what to expect. It is like midwifing my own birth. An odd gestation.

You stand beside me, anticipating every detail of what will develop, each feature of my becoming.

As a haze forms on the negative plate, I am ever-imminent, ever-
Augustine, trapped in limbo, on the verge of emerging. My features
flare into focus, intact, like a woman delivered of the womb fully
grown. Athena from her father's head. I from yours.

The manifestation so miraculous that I swoon.

In the dream, I awake in a room covered wall to wall with my own
image. Augustine sleeping, standing, falling. I glimpse sections of my
body that I have never been able to see until now—walking through
the room, dizzied with myself—there is so much to see. It is like a
city that I have no hope of exploring before I die. These visions of
myself through someone else's eyes.

And I tell M, there must be thousands of them, amassed in the dark-room—a legion of Augustines, unblinking. Imagine them—their immutable bodies, their unwavering stares. An Augustine to occupy the camera's every eye. Enough to overwhelm even the most intrepid observer.

I realize that these are the camera's only equals.

Devoid of daughters, I am rich in sisters—spinsters sown in a sterile womb.

They have developed in darkness, cultivating the power of malignancy. My cancerous, cadaverous selves, my *soeurs de coeur*. Fe-verish and dreaming, waiting for someone to stir them from their somnolence.

Perhaps it is time to reclaim them, this phalanx of harpies, these furies. Perhaps it is time to bring our weight to bear.

I become a thief in the darkroom, sneaking inside at unappoint-ed hours, slipping the curtain aside. The photographs strung like nightflowers on a reddening vine. Dark oak drawers left open and unlocked. I seize dozens of pictures, shoving them into my pockets.

Under my sheets, I assemble my body piece by piece, laying the photographs out across the mattress. Sleeping with this self who is no longer self, this stolen Augustine, secreted away. Pressing my cheek to her collodion cheek—Augustine, *ma chérie*, it is only a matter of time now, I say. And she stares at me wild-eyed, open-mouthed, her face as flat as a dream.

In *la chambre stéréoscopique, la chambre à coucher*, I hum tunes, tell tales. As I move with a languor meant, one by one, to lull the lenses to sleep.

Nature Morte

IN THE STUDIO AT NIGHT, he divests her of images, eager to increase the rate of reproduction, to complete *l'Iconographie*. The manuscript viable, if he can bring it to term.

He directs her glances, tells her how to focus her eyes in the frame. He says, look, don't stare—a stare presents too much hardness. His voice impatient. His hand waving next to the camera in an attempt to distract her from its sumptuous but empty gaze.

Like a saboteur, she baffles the lens, shifting her body to deflect focus. She preens and postures, pretends to brood. When I am bored, she tells him, I have only to make a red bow and look at it. And she twines crimson, vermillion, scarlet ribbons in her hair. Ties them to her neck until she is like an exotic bird, ruby-throated.

He uses "guillotines" to shorten the exposure time—the rapid drop-shutters shaving off slivers of seconds with their circular blades. Removing a ribbon from her neck, he is reminded of Marey, who tethered birds to lengths of string and then ushered them aloft in front of the lens. Determined to document the workings of pinions and feathers, the extraordinary anatomy that could allow an animal to take to the air. Each movement broken down into milliseconds, each image viewed in quick succession allowing a recreation of flight.

He copies Marey's methodology, but the sequences fail to elucidate, her seizures growing enigmatic like movements once seen in dream. Her arms performing full circumductions, her torso twisting past the limitations of muscle and spine. It is as though physiology does not exist. Or as if she, at least, is exempt from its laws.

The farther he pursues hysteria along its twisting path, the more distant his accomplishments feel. He has lived long enough to see each of his endeavors lauded as a success. He has been declared the founder and father of neurology. What guarantee does he have that he can rear another child to maturity, especially a concept as troublesome and obstinate as this? He is just as likely to leave it behind as a failure, fatherless and unfulfilled, the type of progeny to seek vengeance, to topple its sire from his throne.

Better to swallow it whole, kill it in its crib. And yet, he cannot abandon the generative urge, the surgeon's imperative to bury his scalpel within the walls of the womb and deliver one final mystery—gleaming, bloody, raging at its emergence into the world.

He poses for his official portrait in a studio along the Champs Élysées, standing as the photographer suggests, with a hand behind his back, the other tucked in his coat, his head turned slightly to the side. Waiting there, preparing for the camera to take the shot, he feels a certain discomfort, a desire to see himself from the outside, to ensure he adequately resembles himself—though he realizes the thought hardly makes sense. He tugs his waistcoat straight, smooths his hair back from his forehead, and fixes his expression. Readying himself for the exposure, for the instant that always comes as a surprise despite the photographer's warning. The gunpowder stench of the flash.

When he is handed the photograph, he can barely recognize the man who gazes back at him, distorted by the accumulation of decades. He would be less startled to see Augustine posing in his place, dressed in his clothing, her face more familiar than his own.

～

We question hysterics because of their own indifference, he tells his audience, because they speak and act out their suffering, abandon themselves to us, to our pleasure. And everything about them is spectacular—their shouts, their shooting pains, their strangulations. They tear at their hair, contort their faces until they resemble true-to-life gorgons, monstrous enough that a glimpse in the mirror could indeed kill them. Yet, the instant an attack ends, they laugh, free of anguish, of affect.

Watching them, we find ourselves at a loss, unsure how the curtain divides us, why we fail to adjust as easily as they—these impassive divas, these divinities. How do we face them? What mask could we wear to equal their own?

As he speaks, he feels pressure building in his temples. Blackness encroaching along the edges of his vision. Turning to the photographs, he can only see their artifice—her stumble transformed into a swagger, her emotions revealed as histrionics. From one picture to the next, her visage stares out at him from the darkness, disfigured by profound grief and ecstatic joy, indistinguishable from the masks of tragedy and comedy that adorn every theatre. He glances surreptitiously at the amphitheatre's sconces as if expecting to see her countenance leering back at him from the corners. The audience looking upward as well, as if sensing a malevolent spirit. Several spectators cross themselves superstitiously, as the men of science snicker.

We devour hysteria with our gaze, he says slowly—trying to ignore a growing tightness in his chest—and hysteria devours our gaze in return. The longer we look, the less apparent the patient's pain becomes, overshadowed by a style that afflicts us physically. Her body draped and cunningly concealed—withholding, even when naked, some essential part of herself. She becomes the one who elicits anguish, rather than suffers it.

The migraine strikes him after the amphitheatre has emptied, obscuring his vision as if the light flashed before to the camera has burned into his irises, flaming with a peculiar sort of phosphorescence. He must make his way back to the study, his hands trailing along the dampened walls of the hallway, his palms sweating. The fantastic play of light like fireworks flickering out before him.

How often has he sketched her field of vision, drawing the dazzling forms of scotomas down to the finest detail—jagged contours that are curled in the shape of his own initial, like a crescent-cut moon or spiny-backed beast. How often has he waited until her headaches have rendered vision impossible and then asked her, Augustine, *dis-moi,* what do you see? Listening as she described garish swirls and chevrons, the delicate ornamentation of a marvelous brocade.

And yet he has never shared the truth: that he knows the sensation personally, suffering the same agonies, the same loss of sight. Those nights he locks himself in the study, his head a crushing weighty orb. The pattern beginning to pulsate, agitated by rapid vibrations and bursts of color, like elements held above a gas flame burning alternately white, yellow, blue, red. He vomits into wastebaskets, into his hands when he must, too afraid to move. Worried that he might back into the edge of his desk or the mirrored surface of the wall like a myopic old man.

Sometimes the migraines last for days. Sometimes hours. He tells no one about these attacks, puts his head on his desk and waits for them to pass. The luminous shape snaking across the darkness of his pupils, like an afterimage of her body twisting on the bed.

$\sim$

In the ophthalmic laboratory, he drains oculi of their vitreous and aqueous humors, observes them pucker inward like rotting fruit, plucked and peeled—sclera scraped away, ciliary muscles torn. Optical nerves floating in clear glass jars like frayed medusas.

Dozens of eyes fill the dissection trays, shedding one or another of their tunics—fibrous, vascular, nervous. The orbs do not maintain their luster. Removed from the sockets, irises dull and corneas glaze; light ceases its refraction. Nevertheless, they remain attentive, an audience of cyclops studying his every experiment.

We can never hope to see through the hysteric's eyes, he lies to the crowd. It is an impossible vision. One that our brains cannot comprehend. Twisted, warped, and vulnerable to the greatest dissymmetry.

$\sim$

He spends hours in the darkroom, staring into vats of chemicals. Eyes red and burning, head pounding from the strain. And he realizes he has run himself into the ground. Late nights at his desk, in the office. The thick cigars. The heavy meals. The lack of movement for hours on end. He touches his heart as if it is a fragile spot, fingering it like a bruise.

Some nights he thinks he glimpses her blurred figure out of the corner of his eye, sees the hem of her nightgown trailing beneath the curtained entrance, a flicker of movement between the screens and scrims. Sightings he knows can only be explained as the product of his exhaustion.

But there are other occurrences—of unpredictable duration—that he cannot as easily explain away. As he agitates the still waters of the developing bath, he glimpses a reflection of her face moments before the image emerges. A premonition he can neither account for nor dispel. Her likeness suspended above the print which darkens in the bath, then blackens due to his distraction. The semblance is, without doubt, a reflection—rippling with the movement of the liquid while the printed picture remains resolute below, as though she is standing behind him, peering over his shoulder, calling the face to the surface. In these moments, he cannot move, cannot turn his head to look for her, the hairs on his neck erect.

He submerges the plates into vats of potassium cyanide, affixing the images, dousing them in the lethal concoction until the double dissipates. Only then is he able to look behind him.

In his dream, she is winged back and front like some parody of angel or witch—wings sprouting from her nipples, a dulled dark red. He removes the camera that he has built to capture dreams—all screws and cranks and turning things—and snaps the shutter until pictures spread outward on the floor or spring living from the lens. The duplicates of her encircling him. Each Augustine dreaming of him dreaming of her until he forces himself awake.

He notices negatives missing, equipment moved that he has not touched, batches of chemicals with labels torn off, as if there is a ghost in the darkroom, a malicious force intent to destroy. He curses the interns for the increasing number of overexposures, the plates cracked and incorrectly inserted, all the indignities of poor preparation. Accusing them of entering the darkroom after hours, without permission, but they respond with curious looks and ready denials, too confounded to be disingenuous. He retreats to his study, embarrassed, tormented by the youthful pity that tinges their eyes.

I return to remove more of your photographs—picking the locks, prying open compartments, until I uncover every one of your hiding places—ruining the hours you have spent furiously reprinting. Days lost in the dark that cannot be recovered.

In private, you interrogate the patients. You accuse me of thievery, sabotage, and I deny every count. But my body almost betrays me. My hand spasming so that my fingers cross—a puerile indication of schoolgirl's guilt. A giveaway. I hide my hand behind my back before you notice.

I grow bold enough to start stealing in the daytime. Until one morning, *Monsieur*, my apron pockets glutted with photographs, faces sticking out of every seam, the drawer almost empty. Until one morning, *Monsieur, Maître*, I hear you in the room next to me, in the studio. I slip stealthily behind the equipment and screens, trying to discover who you are photographing, my fingers stained with silver nitrate. And it is then that I see him, your subject, his head propped on the platform, positioned in front of the lens.

I have seen him before, in the amphitheatre, his cranium too heavy to hold upright. His face burst into a featureless double— discolored, rancorous—a tumor so large that he appeared double-headed, tissue purpled like an abrasion. In the amphitheatre, you displayed him before the crowd, the monstrous mass cupped in your hands as you tried to bear its weight, to keep him sitting upright. You resembled a boy holding a plum, contemplating its ripeness, deciding which part to bite.

Now, you have taken the entire fruit. Shredded arteries fringing his neckline like living roots, his tongue lacerated between his teeth, his eyes open, the tumor glaring from one side of his face. *Maître,* how heavy was his head when you plucked it from the branch? Did your hands shake when you cut the stem, when you placed his head on the platform but left his body behind like detritus—the only part of him not deformed?

You wanted the disease, the abnormality.

I scream so loudly that you turn to look, quickly covering him with a cloth so that he is gone when I glance again. You rush toward me, reaching out to steady me. You say it was a hallucination. You tell me it must have been an aftershock, a visual default. But I saw him, *Maître,* beheaded in the very spot where I am sitting now—clamped in place because I will not stop screaming. I try everything I can think of to break free from you, to escape this butcher's block, the blood still on it. Biting, spitting, hitting, until the rigor sets in, my hands clasped around my throat, tighter than an iron brace.

Only then do you notice the photographs bulging from my pockets. Immobilized, I am caught red-handed. The realization of my crime stunning you for a moment, before your befuddled stare turns to a look of condemnation, conviction.

There will be no trial, no opportunity to offer a defense, to present mitigating circumstances. You have passed judgment upon me, and I can only await the sentence—a thief on the chopping block. Your cool breath slicing my skin like a scalpel. And then, I am a woman with her throat cut, trying to hold shut the wound, to seam the slit before the blood runs out. I am Medusa with her crown of snakes, the camera's mirrored lens refracting my gaze, making it so easy for you to move closer to me, to strike me down. My head the aegis you hold in front of you, framed. The drops of blood forming worms as they fall. Purpled, sightless creatures, crawling into the jagged cavern of my neck, burrowing until they reach my heart—still busy pumping blood to a head that is no longer there.

I can feel my pupils constricting millimeter by millimeter, like lenses dialed down to their narrowest aperture, then hooded black.

Pièce à Conviction

I AWAKE TO WET, heavy whiteness covering my body, dripping into my eyes, my mouth. I glimpse you above me, body blurred but unmistakably yours. Almost immediately, you lower my eyelids, fingers pressing them closed—a doctor's pronouncement of death—and I am awake but in darkness, the coating hardening around me, pinching my skin, adhering to the hairs on my arms, legs, groin. Minutes or hours later, I cannot tell which, someone knocks on my sternum and I echo hollowly, the sound rebounding, but muffled. The knuckles striking centimeters above my skin, yet never making contact. Blocked by something rigid as a shield, as a chitinous shell. I am encased. Air enters the narrow hole hollowed out between my lips. Your fingers no longer on my eyelids. I do not feel your hands anywhere. Though I hear palpations, like the footsteps of insects, passing over me. I'm afraid they will find their way to my mouth, block my airway, enter under my skin. Devour me.

It is as if I've awakened inside my own grave, or inside the body of another.

You tell me, Augustine, we are making a mold of you. But the words do not make sense to me, bringing to mind only decay. Only later do I understand that I am to become my own reliquary.

While you wait for the plaster to dry, you tell me stories. I strain to hear you, sealed inside the sculpture you have made of me. You tell me the history of the asylum in the years before I arrived, in the years before either of us existed. Back to its beginnings. The roots of the buildings dug in deep below us. The tales are like nightmares. Stories in which limbs are lopped and hewn. Fables without a moral. Accounts that end too soon.

You ask me, Augustine, have you heard this tale? And knowing I cannot answer, you begin to speak.

You describe the *cellules* in which the madwomen slept, manacled and chained. Cages that resembled animals' stalls. The straw raked out only once a week. The reek of it. The filth. And below the cells, you say, drawing closer so that I can hear your words more clearly, below them, Augustine, were pits in which the worst were kept. And every night the rats would gnaw the women's eyes, until each of them was blinded, and half their faces gone.

Your words form images behind my eyelids, project them onto the bare plaster beyond, like a slideshow cast on the asylum walls. The Salpêtrière, a history lesson. I picture you raising your pointer, ready to instruct.

You begin with the Convulsionnaires of Saint-Médard. The most bloody. The most bizarre. Telling with relish how the women dragged their dead deacon behind them on his funeral bier, beating their chests. Their cheeks riven with scratches. Their breasts battered. And one by one, the mourners appear before me in mute processional, covered in wounds. They gather at the grave site, clumps of hair matted in their hands—patches torn out with the scalp still attached. They stoop to eat the earth around the tomb, succumbing to ecstasies, flinging themselves to the ground. Their bodies prostrate before the grave, flailing into seizure. The women bark and mew, leap into the air, strike themselves with axes, spades, hammers, swords. Showing one another how they do not bleed. They twist their nipples with pliers, stick their breasts with pins, until they look like barbed and armored beasts.

They were all imprisoned here, you say, and I can tell you are smiling. The tone of your voice sonorous, as if suppressing a laugh. The king heard about their goings-on and locked them all away. A few of the women tossed in the cells retained only their heads and torsos, having performed the most extreme amputations. When the rats would come, you murmur, the women could not protect themselves.

You rise abruptly, chair legs squeaking against the floor. I hear you moving about the room, pacing. When you fall silent, I cannot tell if you have left. When you speak again, your voice startles me, echoing in the covered drums of my ears.

The Comtesse de la Motte, you announce imperiously, as if you are presenting a royal figure to the room rather than simply starting another story. The Comtesse, you say, the infamous Lady of the Diamond Necklace, downfall of queen and cardinals, was condemned here, sentenced to be whipped and branded. Of course, at that time the Salpêtrière served merely as a bastion of punishment. Science had yet to open its enlightened eye inside these halls.

Before long, the Comtesse managed to escape by disguising herself as a man. She fled to London and penned her scandalous memoirs alleging sexual encounters with the queen. But she never forgot her time here. It is said that when the tax collectors rode up to her estate, she thought the carriages had been dispatched to deliver her to the Salpêtrière. She threw herself from the window, Augustine, rather than return.

I watch as her body hits the ground, inches in front of my closed lids. The noise of it otherworldly. Jagged bones burst through the skin, grey matter spattered on grass. Her face, however, is unblemished, pristine. Blue fractures ringing her broken neck like an ornate, bejeweled collar.

I want to linger with her awhile, know from the twitching of her lips that she has secrets still to tell me. Instead, you rush hurriedly along in your history, flicking the plaster on my forehead to make sure I am paying attention.

During the Revolution, you explain, the iron gates couldn't hold back the crowd—a mass of men wielding sabers, hatchets, mallets. By the time it was over, forty-five madwomen lay massacred. The courtyard clotted with gore. Women's heads impaled on the gates.

The haematic scene congeals before me. Men throwing themselves upon the dying women, raping them. Everywhere the sound of sinew tearing, the gush of ventricular flow. The air smells of carnage, flesh clipped and trimmed as the men claim their souvenirs—an ear, a nipple, a lacerated hand. When the courtyard is once again devoid of men, the animals emerge, crawling with their bellies low to the ground. Crows land on the bodies, burrow their beaks deep into sockets and innards, flocking over the corpses until the women resemble black-winged and bloodied angels. Dogs snap up meat in their slavering jaws.

So much for freedom, you say, so much for revolution. It is a base and brutal history we trail behind us, Augustine, teeming with ghosts and crimes unavenged.

When the tales end, you tell me you are leaving. *Bonsoir,* you say, *beaux rêves.* I can do nothing, say nothing, to stop you. Sealed in my stiffened sarcophagus long after the plaster has dried.

No theft or sabotage seems worthy of such a sentence, *Maître,* that you would leave me here. Motionless. Mute. Like a body abandoned to the grave after the mourners have gone. The self still cognizant, still conscious, trapped inside that loneliest and most inhospitable of homes.

Unseen, the room echoes unnaturally, taking on an unsettling calm. And I long for your company then, the cruel cut of your mouth.

The hours in which you do not arrive are unbearable. The silence breeding waking nightmares. The space around me infected by hallucinations. Festering. In my mind's eye, the room is replete with darkness. Black, three-legged beasts lurk in the doorway, hunched and ready. Rats carapaced in the sable shells of sea creatures ruffle their wings and trill a strange, unsoothing sound.

In the gloaming, my plaster body emits a dim luminescence. Men with dull yellow eyes emerge from underneath the bed. Like moths, a circle of them gathers round me. When the men speak, their mouths emit fire, scorching the air with bursts of flame that burn black and jagged, serrated like teeth. Their tongues will char me where I lie. I do not expect to live through the night.

The creatures scatter the second they hear you coming. I sense them sidling away like crabs, crawling into unlit corners. You strike the casting with something sharp, and I cringe, mistaking the sound of the chisel for the crackling of flames.

When you break open the plaster shell, I emerge chastened. Muscles weak from so little movement. Eyes intolerant of light. Like a cicada summoned from dormancy—vulnerable, naked—I cling to what is closest to me. Your wrinkled skin scabrous like bark.

You pull away, leaving me curled on the ground, larval, formless. And I cannot face you, *Maître,* I do not dare.

In the morning, I am hauled onstage like a criminal presented to the crowd for further punishment. You do not look at me. You do not speak to me. It is as if I have disappeared from sight, as if the earth has swallowed me up and I exist now only as an apparition, so easy to see through, so easy to look beyond.

The interns apply plaster, starting at the crown of my head, coating my eyelids, obscuring the audience behind a curtain of white. They stop at the neckline, my body exposed, bare to the skin. My face masked.

I stand on the boards, a victim hooded for execution. Around me, the murmurs of the crowd swell and subside. The mob impatient in its bloodlust, anxious for the spectacle to unfurl.

Patience, you declare to them, to me, to all of us. Patience.

You commence the lecture, raising your voice to be heard. Your words animate the audience, incite the crowd. But as the paste sets, the sentences grow muffled and indistinct, swelling into a surging, tumultuous drone, only the tone of which is audible.

Midway through the lesson, you remove the mask, the plaster ripping eyelashes and hairs from my face, tearing at the soft lobes of my ears. The applause of the audience strikes me like a series of backhanded slaps. With each clap, I jerk and blink, my eyes assailed by intermittent bursts of light.

Once my pupils adjust, I see that you are staring straight at me. In your hand, you hold a duplicate of my face, concave and bloodless. You look from her to me, projecting your words beyond us, into the crowd. But your mouth, close to our plaster ear, delivers its message directly.

Hysterics offer themselves up to us like relics abandoned, you proclaim. Their bodies goods to dispose of, granted to us even in death. They entrust to us the art of preservation, restoration. And we decide how they will be remembered. If and when they will be resurrected. We, and we alone, you say, your voice low and threatening, decide whether the patient will be immortalized or left in the ground to rot.

M insists that I must escape, that your cruelty will only escalate, and I reluctantly agree. I cannot imagine leaving these halls, stepping down from the stage, any more than you can, *Maître*. But I have felt the power of your attention, and nothing can withstand it.

Between sculpting sessions, I try to remain malleable. I stretch and flex, attempting to dispel the atrophy that has settled into my limbs. At times you scrutinize my eye as if you would like to see behind it—behind the pupil, iris, retina—to see through my vitreous humor and thus usurp my gaze.

I allow you to mistake my acquiescence for surrender. Your threats growing more pronounced even as your voice betrays a brittleness, the stridency of a man forced to resort to increasingly desperate measures. You raise the stakes vertiginously, not yet aware that you have unveiled yourself.

There can be no more doubt. We are engaged in a battle of wills now, a contest of captivation in which one of us will lose our head.

Rédaction

HE RESTORES ORDER TO THE DARKROOM, tucks the photographs back in their folios, erases all evidence of sabotage, and does not raise the subject again. Unable to denounce her duplicity without revealing himself as victim. Instead, he alters events, recounts only an edited version of their encounter, with details redacted and concealed.

There are occasions in which the practice of postmortems can spawn complications and problematic encounters, he tells the audience. Augustine, for example, entered the studio unannounced one day and saw the severed head of a former patient being photographed. The sight produced a most decisive effect upon her, leaving a violent impression that manifested itself in her attacks. Quite simply, she would not let go of her neck. The powerful tetany lasted for hours, until well after we had stopped documenting her reaction—its intensity amplified, perhaps, by the fact that we were photographing her upon the same platform where we had placed the body part. The head, of course, had long since been removed. From the platform.

He chuckles along with the audience, but his face is fixed in a grimace, not a grin.

The revision rebuilds her confidence as she realizes she will not be called to public account for her theft. Her initial pleas—that he return the photographs—morphing into requests, then demands. Her ultimatums backed by an undertone of threat, as if she knows they share secrets he doesn't want exposed.

Despite her insistence, he refuses to allow her back into the darkroom. Forcing her to attend sessions in the *atelier de moulage* instead, knowing how much she dislikes the moldings, the hours spent encased.

The room so silent during these sessions that he can almost forget she is there, centimeters below his fingers, a fossil encrusted, petrified. The chaos of her body finally contained.

If he could, he would curtail all contact with her and study her duplicates instead—the sleek, flattened doubles and their pale plaster twins—so much more malleable than she is, with her mercurial moods, her outbursts.

In the amphitheatre, he finds himself reciting the tale of Pygmalion. The sculptor was determined to live life as a celibate, he tells the audience. The young man was repulsed by women's vices and wicked ways. To alleviate his loneliness, he carved a woman out of alabaster, the epitome of virgin beauty—a semblance so flawless that she seemed alive. The sculpture was a masterpiece, an artwork that concealed its own artifice: wholly his own creation and yet as visceral as any work of nature. He named her Galatea and soon fell in love with his counterfeit maiden, caressing her flesh until he no longer felt stone under his fingertips, but skin that he feared he might bruise. He brought her presents to please girlish tastes: speckled shells and polished stones, amber beads, talking birds, and flowers of varied hue. Dressing her in flowing garments, sliding rings on her fingers, earrings in her ears, pearls round her neck. Tying colored ribbons at her bosom. He strung tinkling bracelets around her wrists and

A

Krulwic

Pickup By:
12/13/2022

ankles so that he would hear her if she began to move. Such finery became her, but she looked most beautiful naked and unadorned, stretched out upon soft, feathered pillows. At night, he prayed to Venus to give him such a woman to share his bed, unable to request what he actually wanted—his sculpted virgin as a living bride. But the astute goddess recognized his true desire and granted it, so that when he next lay with Galatea, her skin seemed to warm, grow pliable, the alabaster yielding to his fingers like wax. Her veins throbbing under his thumb.

As Charcot speaks, he slips inside the sculptor's skin, feels himself carving alabaster hip bones, cutting through stone, sees Galatea blushing before him, opening her timid eyes at the very moment she is no longer virgin, but wife, awakening to the stab of penetration before she's even seen her husband's face.

At the Salpêtrière, we encounter an entirely different dilemma, he muses to the audience, modulating his voice like a man deliberating in the solitude of his study. Preferring the statue, what do we do when she demands to be a living self?

He dedicates a private museum to Augustine in an annex off the studio which no one ever sees. He hangs religious artworks alongside the photographs, pairing the holy with the hysteric to form his own iconography. Her plaster limbs displayed like relics in the corners of the room. He furnishes the annex with a desk and a cot, covering the low, domed ceiling with pictures of her.

He falls asleep contemplating the articulation of her wrist in plaster replica, a sculpted hand cupped between his palms until he can almost believe it is hers, living, wincing, under the press of his flesh.

He spends hours examining the moldings, pouring over the photographs, struggling to see them as a stranger might, to envision them anew. He watches freckles emerge and recede, moles blossom like mushrooms along the damp hollows of her collarbone, lines spread like fissures across her plaster face. And the memory returns to him, unbidden, of that moment in the darkroom, photographs protruding from her pockets, the expression on her face as the tetany set in—the horror of a woman one stroke into her own beheading. The pressure with which she gripped her throat, leaving a necklace of bloody crescent moons behind, a perforated line gouged by her fingernails. How, having overcome his shock, he stared at those marks for days, imagined taking his scalpel to them, completing the incision.

And he wonders, what would his life be without Augustine? Who would he be, and would it be enough?

In his dream, she enters the annex dressed in a corset and full-length skirt, her breasts swelling from the constriction of the bodice. She removes a scalpel from the cleft of her bosom and draws it across the satin side-seam, extracting the whalebone stays one at a time, placing them on the bed like a set of ribs removed from her torso. She slices the ribbon laces until she stands half-naked, her skin marked and scored by the corset along each intercostal. Slipping the skirt from her hips, she runs the dull side of the blade from navel to neck, before flipping it over, cutting along each indentation. She reaches inside herself and pulls out her ribs, spreading them at his feet, the blood running down her chest like the tassels of a scarlet shawl, parting around her pubis, spilling off the sides of her hipbones. She carves a delicate Y—the top of which spans her clavicle—and opens her flesh like a blouse, revealing the cavity of her chest with her heart still palpating inside, suspended within a fretwork of veins and arteries. He is tempted to cup it in his palms, but he remains motionless, muscles rigid, as she brings the scalpel to her hairline, down past her ears, tracing the shape of a mask along the contours of her face. She presses her fingers into the seam on her forehead, prepares to peel.

Out of the corner of his eye, he sees the plaster limbs shudder and stir from their resting places, shuffle toward him—feet arched like inchworms, hands crawling finger over finger to reach him, clambering onto his torso, tearing at his skin until they reach his heart, clench it like a vice.

He awakes to a crushing pain in his chest, pulse weak and irregular, bedsheets plastered to his sweaty face like a shroud. Between spasms of vomiting, he gasps for air, stumbles to the washbasin, plunges his hands and then his head into the water. This is no night terror, no attack of nerves or collapse brought about by overwork. It is the onset of the failure that will be his death. The awareness strikes him with a sudden and sickening finality, as he recalls symptoms and portents that have been accumulating for months. He staggers back to bed and curls into a fetal position beneath the sodden sheets, terrified he will not survive the night.

The next morning, he prescribes himself a regimen of digitalis and dogbane, cancelling his lectures for the week without explanation. He shuts himself in the annex, waiting for the physical lethargy to subside, his mind struggling to grasp the magnitude of the catastrophe confronting him—everything he might be forced to leave behind, unanswered. Picturing other men's hands cutting her open, laying her bare.

He does not mourn the loss of personal attachments—his family, his few friends. Nothing feels as real as his life inside the asylum. The world beyond its walls is a lackluster imitation of the vitality within. The people who know him, whom he knows, they will also die;

everything made of flesh will be forgotten. Who knows this better than him? There is only one route to immortality and it lies in the pages he has yet to pen, the record he has yet to complete. Surely he has earned the right to finish them. Surely he deserves a sliver of knowledge in exchange for a lifetime of seeking.

He tells himself that he has not come this far in order to fail, that fate cannot be so cruel. But his ruminations are tinged with bitterness and regret. With the growing conviction that, poised on the threshold of discovery, he will be denied his final crowning success.

He returns to work the moment he is able, spreading the leaves of his manuscript out before him like entries in a mourner's book, assembling chapters and volumes, noting the crucial material that is still missing, the assertions that lack documentation—the gaps yawning wide as chasms.

Above his desk, he hangs a framed quotation: *man is in the hands of the gods like a fly in the hands of children—they play with it until they crush it.*

At night, he closes his eyes, tries to imagine nothingness, to keep the field of his vision black, empty, to feel his body engulfing him, engulfing itself, to experience death. To accept it. But he cannot stop pictures from forming—dreams, semblances, manifestations his mind can grab onto.

Feeling his body failing in the darkness, her figure appears before him, and he perceives he will find no peace. He has been ruined by his compulsion to see, consumed by this curiosity that is also a curse.

And he thinks of the time he has wasted—each second of which he would do anything to regain.

∞

He hides the signs of his illness for as long as he can, from the interns, from the audience, from Augustine. Observing her from a perch grown ever more precarious.

As the days pass, he realizes he could live for months, perhaps years. There is no certainty as to when the end will come, only that it is approaching. The thread of his life has been measured, the spool diminished, but its remaining length is obscured from view as it always has been. Only now, he can feel it fraying.

He recalls paintings of the three fateful sisters, the Moirai, with their spindle, rule, and shears, but in their place he pictures Augustine, sisterless and vengeful, a length of golden cord stretched taut in her hands. He can feel it tugging behind his ribs, one of many veins far too easy to sever.

In the amphitheatre, he invokes the most violent attacks, wonders whether they will tear her apart. Like a reverse bacchanal. Destroying the one who is seen rather than the one who sees. He envisions her final paroxysm with a pitch of elation that approximates grief, his throat catching, his eyes moist.

Hysteria forces us to fear our bodies, to feel the shame of their lewd impulses, to flee from a vision of our death, he tells the audience. How are we to comprehend a disease that both denies and courts mortality?

The hysteric indulges her body to the point of its impending extinction, driven to extremes that the physical self cannot endure. Perhaps we are wrong to extend her suffering, to delay discoveries that belong in the annals of medicine—their delivery long overdue.

He performs autopsies on the busts, breaking open brittle chests and abdomens, splitting apart plaster skulls. He cuts limbs from her body, hacks and hews, truncates her arms at the wrists, then again at the elbows. Watching the castings crumble at the edges like bones ground to dust. Her feet dismembered pedestals, supporting nothing. He disarticulates joints as gently as a man might help a woman undo the clasp of her necklace, his hand lingering lightly against the smooth slope of her neck.

He surrounds himself with the moldings he has made of her, and duplicates born from those. Each sculpture growing more fantastical —winged like butterflies or possessed of extra appendages and breasts. The horned Augustine, the child Augustine, the saint. He manipulates the molds and recasts the plaster, posing her in every permutation. Augustine the erotic—plaster hand between her legs, plaster head flung back, her body damp and lissome. He strokes her contours, but her skin always stiffens and sears, no matter how often he moistens the materials, as if she is hardening herself against him, shutting him out. He sits beside her, waits for the moment when the statue will waken, her skin warm to the touch.

During the day, he examines patients in almost complete silence—tapping his hand on the table. Requesting only the slightest of movements, that a reflex be checked, a sentence of speech uttered, a sensory response confirmed. His eyes barely discernible—the dark sockets, the dull gleam of iris. Each patient in silence brought to him, in silence dismissed. But in the hours when he is alone, surrounded by portraits that work their way into his dreams, he is given over to her more than ever. Sleeping in the hidden annex, entombed with her image—her body suspended somewhere above him, somewhere below.

IV.

Confiances

M AND I ATTEMPT TO SOLIDIFY a strategy for escape—pillaging plots from myths, novels, histories that you yourself have narrated. I rule out one idea after another. M worries I have lost my resolve. But I am merely seeking a satisfying denouement, testing every plot for the aura of authenticity.

One day, you enter the studio while we are conspiring, caught up in the thick of conversation, so that we do not notice your presence at first. Until I see you reflected in M's irises, moving up behind me, and I freeze in fear.

I stand up quickly to distract you, afraid that you have noticed M or overheard something to raise your suspicions. Instead, you grab an implement, prepare to leave. And I realize that I need not have worried. I will never be more than an object to you, an instrument of inquiry.

It occurs to me that this is your fatal flaw. For in this space, objects are imbued with incalculable power, an intrinsic ability to enchant. And I am the most formidable object of all—stunning, hypnotic, a magnetic body possessed of a terminal attraction.

The attack strikes you in public, in front of the audience, the spasm prolonged, protracted. Followed by a distinct fibrillation in the chest, a fluttering I feel all the way down to your fingertips. Your hand, holding mine, preparing it for the plaster, grasps tighter and tighter until I think the blood will stop flowing. The ends of my fingertips purpled. The entirety of your face a pale and anguished white.

I can feel it in your grip, this symptom of your death.

My chest also constricting.

I have been preparing to battle a titan, but what M has told me is true—you are merely mortal, *Monsieur*. No different from the rest of us. And I am disappointed despite it all, stricken by a feeling of loss.

Maître, I think, must you end up just a man?

You dismiss the concerns of colleagues, scold the interns when they suggest a doctor's exam, shrug off the entire episode as a case of acute indigestion. You nearly convince yourself with your certainty. But you do not let them listen to your chest. Knowing what they will discover—the insufficient arteries, the edema.

M urges me to take advantage, to expose your weakness publicly. For reasons that I cannot explain, the thought of doing so seems the most egregious violation, like a protégé turning against her mentor, or a devotee against her fallen god.

Instead, I cultivate your dependence. I act as your assistant behind the scenes, never letting anyone notice how you balance your weight on my shoulder, how I stall during demonstrations to let you catch your breath.

Together, we craft a convincing illusion.

I do not lower my guard. I watch your hands as though they are dangerous instruments. I think, if I had even one of those limbs, what I could do. And I study you. And I learn.

A procedure like this cannot be rushed, I tell M, it must be executed with absolute precision.

I do not share the details—knowing M will not understand the risks I intend to incur. I am certain, though, that they are worth taking.

I have conceived of an ending to our story, *Monsieur*. If it comes to fruition, I will make you an accomplice to your own undoing. If it fails, the fight will have been formidable, a contest of equals brought to a fitting conclusion, a *coup de grâce* of staggering proportions. That—if nothing else—you have earned.

As if compelled, you begin to confide in me. Often the words you speak are inconsequential, but your tone carries the weight of confession, of sentiments that can no longer be kept inside, expressed begrudgingly as if torn from your throat. They emerge ragged and bloodied, guttural.

Some nights, you come to me with the expression of a man famished for flesh, eying my body ferociously like a fiend impatient to collect his due. A beast long of claw and sharp of fang. Feral. Starving.

At other times you approach furtively, gently touching the bones of my face, my jaw, my neck. Your gestures tranquil, almost reverent. And it is only when you turn to leave that I glimpse the scalpel clenched in your fist.

Perhaps it is the way the blade shakes in your hand, the look of exhaustion in your eyes, but I do not fear for my welfare. From a distance, your face is like a mask, impenetrable, aloof. But up close,

Maître, there is that movement of the muscles you make when you are in pain, a lowering at the corners of your mouth, a tightness in the cheeks. There are subtleties of expression which I have learned to discern. Moments when I see that you need me perhaps more than you ever have.

You allow your imagination to become unbound, and I encourage you, pushing you toward the margins of scientific study, responding to your most outrageous ideas with alacrity. It is so easy to lead you where you already want to go, up to the edge and then past it. Like the audience, you are searching for a spectacle, something you can surrender to, an excuse to let yourself be overwhelmed. I will act as that intoxicant, *Maître.* It is the role I was born to play.

I observe your rage coupled with fatigue, the frustration with which you anticipate a finale that you cannot orchestrate. How desperately you hope to dazzle them all—the students, the cynics, your most fervent disciples. In truth, we are seeking the same end—to overthrow the established order, to invoke the violence of epiphany—neither of us the sort to settle for a minor revelation.

   Quel dommage, Monsieur. We could have formed a partnership for the ages, if only we had learned to share the stage.

You seek me out with increasing frequency—bearing gifts and spirits, all manner of inebriants, incentives. And I accept them like a woman wooed.

   You ask me to stand, and I do so, ask me to speak my name, and I do, wondering why you have not always approached me like this, with deference, respect, a polite request. Something I am more than willing to respond to. You use the words *cooperation, collaboration.* I insist you begin with contact, your fingers brushing my eyelids, your hand resting on the crown of my head. It has been so long since you touched me with tenderness, *Maître*. I can see that it pains you, but an act of enchantment, after all, must be earned.

In return, you request wonders, repetitions, dispossessions, working toward a protocol you can flawlessly reproduce on the stage. You trill, Augustine, like I am a bird clenched in your fist. Illuminating the entire room to stun me into somnolence.

You move faster in your work than you ever have. Stricken by migraines, arthritis, bouts of angina—a man punished by wrathful deities.

There are times when you fall fainting into my arms. Moments when you are most yourself. When you are most my own. Nights when the pain has taken nearly everything you can see and smashed it.

You whisper, Augustine, seize for me, and it is as if the limberness of my body somehow loosens your own. Bit by bit, the weariness recedes until you glide through the room like a conductor, raised beyond the ache of bones into the realm of art. Operatic. You say my seizures are like evenings at the symphony, listening from the darkened box when the lights go down—your arms outstretched at the beauty of it all as you name each note, each phrase, each *entr'acte*, the *repos*, the *grands tableaux*, and I watch your long fingers extended, the metronome of your mouth spelling out every measure, directing my movements as only you can. *Maître. Maestro.*

When I drop to the floor, you rest beside me. Your shoulders drawn toward your chin, your sharp nose stooped and tucked downward like a bird attempting to hide its head in its wing. And for a moment, I wish I was old and birdlike, cradled in the crook of your arm. But that would never be possible for us. I am the support. The arch leaned against. The body bearing the burden of each of your conjectures.

I learn to anticipate these unplanned intermissions, interruptions in which equilibrium is reversed, undone. Your stance unsteady, your arm cramped at your side. This is what you fear: to be left feeble, blinded. And worried by the amount you can no longer see, you turn to trancework, to the realm of the invisible, in which even the bodies of old men conduct a current strong enough to break my body in two.

I exert just enough power to keep you off balance without tipping my hand. For an observant man, *Maître,* there is so much that you refuse to recognize. You lead me through an array of basic commands, act out my movements as if you are my mirror, and by the time you decide to make the hypnosis public, you fully believe it is your choice.

Leçons

He visits fairground booths where mesmerists bend minds and bodies to their will in front of clamorous and jeering crowds. The subjects given over wholly to their enchanters, whose creations they become, like living automatons abandoned to trance, capable of the most prodigious achievements. And he recognizes there is no other way forward. He must present his findings and enlist her cooperation. He must prepare her for the performance of a lifetime.

He hosts a colloquium at the asylum, gathering together rivals, critics, luminaries in the field. He masks his uncertainty by embracing it, daring them to challenge him. Feels the vertiginous rush of a man perched on a precipice who chooses to lean forward.

He begins by introducing the processes of magnetism and metallotherapy to the crowd. He covers her skin in precious metals, slips silver under her tongue, lays gold across her belly. Adorning her like a Hindu deity. Copper pieces in her palms. Her collarbone inlayed with plates of platinum. A bronze coin resting on her forehead in place of a third eye.

Each hysteric has her own metallic predilection, he tells the audience, an element to which she responds particularly. We learn through trial and error which substance has a strong effect.

Gold, he says, is Augustine's mineral of choice.

In the future, metal will be transformed into internal medicine—soluble ore ingested, injected, solid plates implanted in the body, aureate rivers in the veins—as effective as any drug. As he speaks, his eyes reflect the glow that the coins cast off her skin, his pupils jaundiced, avaricious. Her image trapped within his irises, glimmering like a vision of what could be—a body gilded, gleaming. A statue for false idolatry, a philosopher's stone.

He excavates like a miner with no light to lead him. Her body plundered by his hands. He tells her, Augustine, you are a rare and auspicious ore.

And for a moment, he forgets to fear that the future will not include him.

To master this disease, he proclaims, we must take risks; we must even apply scientific rigor to that which, until now, has inhabited the realm of superstition. I am talking, ladies and gentlemen, about hypnosis. By experimenting privately with this method, I have discovered the means to produce hysteria's morbid phenomena at will, to simplify the symptomatic tableaux, which is far too profuse when spontaneous. In doing so, we can purify the disease, refine it to its most sublime state.

I have been reluctant to bring this revelation before you, to lay public claim to such a tainted art.

He scours the crowd for skeptics, sees his colleagues exchange nervous glances. Several rise from their seats and stalk out of the room, muttering aspersions. But he has already gone too far to turn back. He can only continue.

We have at our disposal dozens of methods to induce trance: the simplest being to take possession of the subject, to take her under your gaze. The patient's eyes grow vague, bloodshot, wet with tears; they close, and then she is yours. She will follow you anywhere without breaking eye contact. If you bend, she bends. If you move forward with a menacing air, she falls backward, straight and rigid, as if felled by the finger of God.

He runs her through the gamut of awakenings and stupors, inducements and delusions, moving from spot to spot on the stage to make her follow.

In the grip of trance, he explains breathlessly, she becomes a prima donna who, in the midst of madness, mistakes the drama she is performing for reality. She can believe herself to be anybody. She will adopt new mannerisms, new memories, to reflect the personality imposed upon her, producing imaginary props or working with what you give her.

He glances out at the audience, sees a hundred eyes wide with astonishment, and cannot tell if they are amazed by the spectacle or aghast at the sight of him. Under the weight of that gaze, he falters.

It is true that we must be her mirror, he stammers, must perform in order to get her to perform. Coupling ourselves so visibly with hypnotized subjects can make us feel the fool. Men like us prefer to work behind the scenes, to keep ourselves out of the limelight.

The hypnotic methodology allows us no safe space. It is pure exposure—blatant, risky, uncomfortable—but capable of manifesting all we have been seeking for so many years.

On stage, he settles into a routine, displaying and hawking his wares, presenting the attacks like a busker at a fair. Rather than eliminating symptoms, he provokes them, drawing them forth when her body will not manifest them spontaneously, inducing hypnotic achromatopsia, stigmata, deliria. Conditions he once intended to cure.

Their performances thrill the audience, evoking the tension of a high-wire act. A delicate balance always on the verge of disaster.

∾

Tuesdays in the amphitheatre, I await the doubt that will be your undoing. Uncertain which raised hand will produce the poisoned blade, which peer will deliver the traitorous blow, but I know it is only a matter of time. The hours I've spent observing your audience, your interns, have not passed in vain. I know what attracts them, repels them. I can see them struggling to maintain faith, the resentment building even as they surrender to the wonders taking place before them.

You can ask a person to relinquish power only so often, *Monsieur,* before he turns on you. That is something I could have taught you.

In the studio, you insist on countless reenactments, long after we have both learned our roles by heart. And I realize the repetition owes less to apprehension than to longing—a desire to remain within the enthrallment, to linger there like a body deprived of resistance, finally granted a moment of rest.

I refuse to allow you time for recuperation. Insisting instead that you keep me entertained, entice me with some new amusement, direct me in a fresh scene. I disappear into character, grow unrecognizable, only slowly reemerge as myself—assuming myriad roles: the penitent, the murderess, the lover, the thief.

I am rewarded publicly for my secretions—coins dropped into my palms, onto my belly, pooling in the humid hollow of my lap.

During attacks, you lavish me with currency. Twenty francs, then one hundred, finally you throw them down by the thousands.

It is not surprising, you tell the audience, that over time we must deposit more capital for the body to proffer the same reward. As investors in this disease, we follow the phenomenon with interest, eager to see where it will plateau, what heights it may obtain. Our experiments yield new paradoxes, unexpected benefits. Note, if you will, how this attack, in full progression, is stopped by gold—the obsession of alchemists throughout the ages, now the hysteric's cure. Even as her spasms subside, the rate of her secretions increases, depositing a wealth of effluvium that we can study at our leisure. This is an asset whose value cannot be overstated, that compounds itself over time.

Your voice shakes with excitement, your eyes surveying the crowd. Too distracted to notice the rapid rate at which the coins disappear—francs secreted away during a deceptive spasm, a well-timed shudder. In my room at night, the lucre amasses in growing piles, glinting eyes in the darkness. Each wink an acknowledgement of my sleight of hand.

Your gaze is so easily diverted. Throwing coins in your wishing well, *Maître*, you do not realize you are funding my escape.

∞

The performances grow increasingly garish, replete with sparklers and gongs, flares and concussions, giant tuning forks that set the entire auditorium atremble.

At times, you tell the crowd, we resemble pyromancers, *artificiers*, igniting magnesium flames and gunpowder, materials more appropriate to the asylum's original purpose, or to that of a theatre. Such displays produce an instantaneous state of lethargy.

In this condition, the hysteric will react to the merest mechanical contact in the same way that a normal subject would respond to an intense electrical shock, you explain. Your touch coursing through every fiber, every follicle, until I am galvanized, conductive.

I grow dazzling, my body radiating light. Flooding the room, blowing out the electric filaments, shorting the sockets. My body a beacon drawing everyone for miles. While they look at me, everything is suspended—their wills, their destinies, their desires, all suspended in the resplendent curve of my back. They stare as if they've been benighted. The striking inflection of my eyes in this trance that is both beneath time and beyond it.

My gaze medusan, freezing everything in sight.

You succumb to my influence as never before. When you run out of scenes to enact, I readily supply them—the sessions shifting subtly so that you are the one following my lead, imitating my movements. Your body stiff and awkward as you struggle to strike poses that I perform so naturally. When I throw myself upward, it is only from the desire to see you follow me in flight. My mockingbird *Maître*, my mimic, my mime.

In the studio at night, you rest your head—which has always held too many ideas—in the palms of your hands. You call me enchantress. *Sorcière*. You say, sublime, Augustine. Augustine, you are sublime. Coming to me night after night like a man possessed.

You turn to me, searching for a sign, a clue, some promise of revelation, and a tremor passes through your limbs. But it is not the palsy that causes you to shake.

Only now do you realize the way in which your body is as convulsive as my own.

You say, Augustine, I am dying. And, *Maître*, there is nothing I can do. For years I have invested in your immortality, believed myself to be contributing to a sacred enterprise destined to survive the ages. In truth, I am tethered to your mortal coil, as you are to mine. The first of us to depart—whether by doorway or by casket—will seal the other's fate, condemn the one left behind to obscurity, irrelevancy, to an unfulfilled existence that will end in an ignominious demise.

I have no intention of being left behind.

Paroles
1881

THE SALPÊTRIÈRE BECOMES KNOWN to some as the capital of prestidigitation, the pinnacle of magic—to others as a freakshow, a city of conmen. Your peers calling you *Monsieur Charlatan* behind your back, mocking your descent from science to subterfuge.

I mark the months with symptoms—spasms, paralysis, the loss of hearing and speech. These intemperate seasons. These lengthened days. Until time consists only of attacks and treatments given. The nights of hypnosis, the hours of ether, the seconds of somnolence, provoked.

When I am bored, I manipulate your charts. Take elaborate breaths. Watch how the lines rise and fall, trying to create a pattern. The ridges of mountains I will climb in order to escape. The curves my body forms in convulsions. I make the lines dance and arc, try to write the beginning of my name. The sharp *A*. The dropped and curved belly of a *U*. But more often, I make the shapes of *M*'s over and over. Breathing in, the sharp upward slant, then two short breaths like pants, a long exhalation. *M*.

And *Maître*, you do not even notice the pattern. Analyzing the dips and rises, never understanding the joke.

M scolds me for my recklessness. But, really, there is no reason—

you are beyond the point of noting all but the most extraordinary indicators, your focus narrowed only upon that which you wish to see.

Piece by piece, I collect men's clothing—first trousers and shirt, then jacket—meeting the guards in the halls at night. Their hands under the skirt of my nightgown as I take one item from each.

I practice pinning my hair up, each pin precisely hidden, until I can do so without looking. It is a show like any other—another pose, another costume change. The *pièce de résistance*, a monocle, which I fit over my eye with the odd feeling of second sight. It has cost me much to manage this. I squint and then let it drop from my eye. It swings back and forth from my breast pocket. When I tuck it away, it presses flat against my nipple, inconspicuous.

In bed at night, I promise M that we will never return to this place, that we will disguise our names and identities. That we will live our lives in secrecy. My voice low, confiding. The features of M's face fading and then reemerging against the white sheets. Irises darkened and shuttered like lenses.

M's mouth opens in warning, but only a series of hisses and clicks emerge. Skin sloughing off as your features coalesce beneath it, *Maître,* beaked and defiant, your gaze transfixing mine as the room reconstitutes itself around us. Revealing the stage lights flickering on the periphery. The spectators shifting in their seats. And I am appalled to find that I cannot stop speaking, answering your questions as if I am a woman with nothing to hide.

In the studio at night, he walks in on confidential conversations between Augustine and her lover—one-sided monologues with crucial information omitted. He is stunned by the intimacy with which she speaks and responds, using tones he imagined were for his ears alone. *M'aimes-tu?* she asks, listening to an answer that he cannot hear. The longing in her eyes causing a clenching in his chest, an envy that erupts into anger. She has found companionship elsewhere—a tangible solace that has been denied to him. Ever the observer, he remains on the outside, neither full participant nor paramour in this threesome she has orchestrated.

He asks her, Augustine, did you ever love me, and uncorks a bottle of amyl nitrate under her nose to elicit a response. And she says, when I saw you were the master, I was afraid, and that was all I could comprehend, your knowledge like a weight that could crush me or spring me from this loaded trap.

He probes the limits of entrancement, checking for weaknesses—elements that break or strengthen the spell. Determined to bypass the need for cooperation, to violate the boundaries of consent. He introduces chloral hydrate, atropine, intensifying the frequency and duration of each trance, striving to show her how completely she belongs to him. But he cannot ignore the palpable presence that stands between them like a barrier. M. The interloper harbored safely in an annex of her imagination that remains beyond his control—a sanctuary to which he has sought entry for so long but has never been admitted.

And inside him, an impulse grows to waylay and then break her will—to take something away from her, something she cannot live without.

The hysteric is a consummate actress, he tells the audience, but she forgets the cardinal rule of the stage: in theatres, trust is established only in order to be broken.

You unleash the greatest conflagration yet, and the blaze blinds us both for a moment, its afterimage forming a shroud between us, a haze that gradually coalesces, thickening into a silvery screen like the surface of a mirror dividing us one from the other.

You approach unexpectedly, from the side, grasping my elbow with an authoritative air, ushering me out of one room and into another—a ballroom of sorts, the gold of your pocket watch glinting off the parquet floor, directly into my eyes. In the glow of the gas lamps, you appear as you must have looked decades ago—your skin cleaved tight to the bone, devoid of wrinkles and bulges—standing erect, body trim and muscular. Even your gaze has changed, filled with a mischievousness that appears only when you are most engaged.

The room is crowded with bodies, figures plucked straight from a lunatics' ball. Dressed in delicate nightgowns and straitjackets that double as waistcoats with flowers pinned to the lapels. There are others present in the crowd, doctors, celebrated guests, whom you greet with a brief nod of the head, your dress shoes clicking a staccato rhythm against the boards.

As we approach the center of the room, you tuck a sprig of lily-of-the-valley into your breast pocket, milky-white bells chiming slightly on their stems. Your arm, tense under mine, pulls me slightly toward you, and the flowers jangle louder, clash with the sounds of instruments now being tuned. Cut-crystal chandeliers catching the light, refracting rainbow patterns on the walls behind us.

A gong echoes in another room and the dancers don their masks, transforming into half-human figures with the faces of foxes, butterflies, birds. In the spirit of the masquerade, you too have transformed, your face that of an owl with a monocle dangling from his left eye, grey feathers having replaced your slicked grey hair. I am the only one in the room without a mask. From our left, a man approaches in the guise of a peacock, his proud display of feathers fanned out around his head so that he appears to have dozens of eyes. It is hard not to stare as he bows to me and offers his hand. I demur, but he soon grows insistent, and I move to your side, reach for your arm. You are engaged in conversation with a wolf in a damask gown, your eyes averted. I turn back to the stranger to make my apologies, which he accepts politely, drawing from his pocket a perfumed handkerchief bordered with lace. I raise it to my nose, breathe deeply, surprised by how strong the fumes are, the fabric impregnated with a sickly sweet odor that seems unsuitable for a refined gentleman. As soon as I lower the cloth, he grabs me, and I'm overcome with revulsion, his fingers scaly and taloned like the claws of a bird.

I turn in your direction, see you disappearing into the crowd, and rush to reach you, pushing aside upholstered chairs and lacquered end tables, while men with the snouts of hounds turn and stare, show their teeth. Their ears pointed forward and alert. The room has begun to smell like a barnyard, the odor of fur and feathers mingling with the scent of cigars and the stench of phosphorous. The dancers' shoes strike the parquet with the hollow clip of hoofs, their laughter transmuted into whinnies, snarls, the snorts of swine. The tassels of the women's shawls resemble tails tumbling from the backs of their skirts. The men look like bats wrapped in their own black wings.

I try not to lose you in the crowd of creatures whirling and heaving around me. There is a sudden surge in the music, and the peacock grasps my hand. I turn to see that his eyes have multiplied, his talons locked around my fingers, his beak sharp and hissing. He catches my gaze and I find that I cannot look away. He leads me to the dance floor. Somewhere a watch ticks close to my ear. The dancers wheel and stomp, surround me in the midst of their stampede. Applause breaks out along the edge of the ballroom and the dancers drop their masks and take their seats, leaving me standing in the center of the stage, an intern clenching my hand in his, as you emerge from the wings and bow, the audience on their feet for a second ovation. On the floorboards, a rag soaked in ether, a scattering of chairs.

I look from face to face, disoriented, until M emerges from the audience, wearing a mask devoid of features and decorations. The expression on M's face, when the mask is lowered, is bereft. And I can see that my inattention has opened a wound. That M cannot understand my desperation to reach you, my distress at being separated from your side.

Later that night, M accuses me of an allegiance to you that I fervently disavow. The allegation lingering like a reverberation in the air.

$\backsim$

You interject yourself between M and I more and more often. Confusing me with your sudden attentiveness, just when I had accepted your indifference.

Sometimes I find myself watching you with the awe of an assistant who does not know your tricks, who does not want to. Recalling the way you once brought me down before you, my body birthing magic in this room.

I try reassure M. Insist that the mutual enchantment is gone, vanished, the apparatus of every illusion easy to see.

In truth, I mistake you for M repeatedly, my thoughts addled by injections, by the ever more elaborate deceptions you employ. Disguising your voice, your countenance, your clothing, turning the trances against me with a masterful hand.

I react like a body deprived of resistance, compelled to comply.

I tell you detail by detail my escape—the costume, the key secreted away and hidden inside the mattress. This I will hold in my mouth like a second tongue, I tell you. I describe every gesture I will use to fool the interns. My mannish walk, my monocle. I tell you I will go to the Bois de Boulogne, where I have walked with M so often, that we will start a revolution, that we will star in it.

M listening from the wings, aghast, as I unravel plot after plot, betray every confidence.

I convince myself I must keep my own counsel, reluctant to share my plans even with M, for fear that it is you, *Maître*, hidden behind M's skin. But M takes my reticence personally. And the fissure between us widens and spreads. Which I realize, too late, has been your intention all along.

One day, you summon me to the amphitheatre, show me an exotic bird tethered to a stand—teal wings, green tail feathers, golden auriculars. It ducks and bobs its crested head, regards me with an intent, reptilian eye. The serrated gape of its beak emitting a screech as you tear out a tail feather. The quill oozing a dark, coagulated ink.

You press the plume into my palm, say, Augustine, *écris tout.* Turning to address the audience as I craft calligraphic flourishes as plumed and lustrous as wingstrokes through air.

The phenomenon of somnambulistic writing is indeed unique, you explain. The sound of my scribbling extending your sentence like a hiss. The patient does not truly author but transcribes, as though her body has become a vessel for our words. She draws no effectiveness from the act, being a mere conduit, almost like the pen itself, an instrument through which our will is made manifest.

We tell Augustine to write, and once she has begun, she is wholly concentrated upon the act, to an unimaginable extent. To test her focus, we yell at her, speak into her ear, move our fingers over her face, going so far as to pry down her lower eyelids and reveal the conjunctiva, and it will not distract her nor disrupt her prose. Even an absence of ink will not stop the flow of her words. If the paper on which she is writing is rapidly removed, she takes no notice and continues on the downstroke of the letter she was in the midst of tracing, only now on the wood of the table.

Once she has finished, she will stop and prepare to reread everything she has written. If we hand her a piece of unmarked paper, she continues to see the invisible text. She will even add periods, commas, accents, dot her *i*'s and cross her *t*'s. If one overlays this page on top of the original, he will find that a horizontal bar, an acute or grave accent corresponds exactly to an unaccented letter or an uncrossed *t* on the inscribed sheet below. This is not an extraordinary result. It can be repeated again and again, in session after session.

Once I start writing, I cannot stop, scrawling until the page is filled, the pen run dry, the desk below me carved and ciphered.

The words pour out of me: confessions, confidences, threats. Sentiments I no longer recognize as my own. I write poems, pledges, contracts lacking only your signature. Promising to abandon myself to you, *Maître,* to be your star once more, your Augustine, if only you too will return to me—devoid of resistance, amorous and enchanting. I lay our complicity bare. Reveal our connivances and counter-offers, our *quid pro quos.* But no one reads my rantings, least of all you.

Instead you play childish games, pulling the paper out from beneath my pen, giving me implements empty of ink, passing blank pages that you instruct me to read. And I repeat each sentence by heart, as if the words are engraved on the backs of my eyelids, etched into my tongue, spit out from some dank and phlegmy organ which has finally been given speech.

It is an incident that leaves M unwilling to speak to me—a quarrel that lodges in the heart, settles like a wedge between us, a splinter working its way through the vein.

M's silence is devastating, the traumatic amputation of a critical limb, a sensory organ. I react with a pitch of resentment that is rooted in the pain of rebuke. The pique of a partner who cannot admit her fault. I say, M, you have no faith in me, no confidence that I know what I am doing. Even as I say this, I know I am acting the fool.

Peine

IN THE FACE OF M's WITHDRAWAL, you make a poor substitute and a worthless confidante—interested only in suggestions you have planted, words you have compelled.

My body rebels like a creek bed run dry, a well exhausted. Your hand between my legs accomplishing nothing. The color rising in your cheeks as you are forced to explain this sudden cessation. This refusal to exude after even the most lurid manipulations.

Hysterics thrive on resistance, you tell the audience. They possess a propensity for "retaining the blood," just as plants in desert regions conserve and pool their water. Some lose their menstruations after a great fright. Others die from a surfeit of platelets, despite more than three hundred lettings. The Convulsionnaires of Saint-Médard refused to bleed even under the blows of swords.

You look at me then, and I wonder if you are armed. If you will split me from sex to sternum, saw me in two. I clamp my thighs together and clench my jaw. My eyes stinging from tears that desiccate before they form.

In bed at night, I confess to empty air, beg for forgiveness, hoping M will hear me and grant a reprieve. I ask, *m'aimes-tu?* But there is no response.

Nightmares clamber forth to fill the void. The deadmen set loose, roaming the wards with their mouths of flame. Mandibles branch from their jaws. Pincers probing the cells, searching for me. The deadmen light their way with uncanny fire. Genitals hanging heavy from their laps or pointing the way like compass needles, divining appendages that lead them onward.

And I whisper, M, these halls are too quiet without you. These silences too infinitely loud. Angry as you are, we are not enemies. We cannot be, or I am damned.

∽

In the amphitheatre, the trances take on an air of recklessness, re-enacting violations, treasons, improprieties. At your suggestion, I pick pockets, slip powder into drinking glasses, plot uprisings.

Is a crime committed under hypnosis a simulacrum of crime or a crime itself? you ask the audience. And how far down the path to delinquency do we dare lead our subject in our quest "just to see"? We can make subjects admit to debts and depravities, eat the vilest refuse, strip to the skin and commit fake crimes with unloaded guns, imitation arsenic, but only if they are willing. They are fully capable of refusing to comply.

Ask yourselves: if a woman, entranced, allows herself to be seduced, is she a loose woman or a woman ravished? If she obeys a command to burn this asylum down with all of us inside, is she responsible for her act?

She must consent at least slightly to every degradation, every seduction, every crime. There is no such thing as absolute, involuntary submission, *messieurs et mesdames,* and thus no complete lack of culpability.

And I wonder, *Maître,* why do you tempt me? What conflagration do you hope to ignite?

I begin to doubt that there is a world beyond these walls, that you are not fabricating its existence, pretending to admit an audience when, in fact, the onlookers are patients, dressed and playing their parts. I have wandered the wards trying to find them, these endless rows of spectators, trying to discover where they sleep, what *atelier* you invent them in.

One day, a woman in furs who is watching our performance winks at me, and I recognize her face from the electrical baths. Your assistants grabbing me before I can run off the stage, into the audience, ready to tear the hat from her head, the dead animal from her neck, to expose once and for all this charade, to prove I am no longer under your sway.

∽

I ask you, *Maître*, what you have done with M? And you smile smugly, say M will not be returning, that it is just the two of us now. You tell me that history is full of jealous spouses. In literature, mythology.

That night I break into the darkroom, tossing aside reams of photographs, peering inside the black bellies of cameras, looking through lenses, searching for M.

I find only versions of myself, pale countenances staring from crepuscular shadows. I whisper, have you seen M? But they remain speechless. Perhaps they have been sworn to secrecy. Perhaps you have torn their tongues out at the root.

Back in my room, I dream of the darkroom on fire—white flames, vats of chemicals burning.

Sweat soaking my pillows and sheets as I wait for M to awaken me, to place a palm on my forehead and whisper, quiet, quiet *ma belle*, everything passes, everything ends.

When morning arrives, I refuse to rise from my bed, to abandon my vigil. You come to my side, coo to me, compliment me. You say, Augustine, your fits are like flowers, continually unfolding—and as you speak, your face softens and I know this must be a dream. Your hands tracing the delicate shapes of blossoms before me in the empty air. You will never be like this. Even in the moments when your hands press below my breast, they will never be this gentle; they will only make me seize.

I cannot forgive you, *Monsieur,* for what you have stolen. There was a time when I would have slit my throat so I could smile at you twice. Now, if I could, I would break the wings of birds, leave their flightless bodies at your feet. I would snap the thigh bones of small dogs just to watch you wince. And still we wouldn't be even, you and I. Still you wouldn't feel half of the pain you have caused me.

She finds new ways to resist him, wresting control of half of her body so that she is split down the center by contradictory suggestions, conflicting commands. The left side of her body turned truly sinister. One eye persistently closed in an insolent wink. He struggles for weeks to eliminate the contracture. Clearly, he says, there is still much to learn about the hypnotic process and its effects upon hysteria. This illness offers itself to us like a sphinx, defying even the most penetrating anatomy.

In the studio at night, he asks the sphinx questions. Lowers himself on belly and knee, requesting clues to the riddle she poses. Angered by her body, by its brilliance.

Her winged back. Her leonine paws.

Around her lie the bodies of the slain, men of name and note who have failed to answer her questions correctly.

He asks her for answers but is only given more seizures. Her semi-smile growing as pronounced as the curvature of her spine.

Long after he has left the room, he wonders what it would feel like—to have her jaws on his jugular, the slow strangulation, her claws sheathed yet sharpened, the feathers of her wings arching above them both like an eagle shrouding its prey.

He waits for daylight, when he can exercise his coldness, his control. Exerting power to see if he still possesses it. Their sessions veer off into increasingly treacherous terrain, perilous expeditions beyond the edge of the map, into the realm of monsters.

She guards every entrance, every exit, indicating in no uncertain terms that the time for guessing is over. He has reached the threshold where she awaits her answer, poised to slay him or leap to her death.

∾

He gathers the interns around him as a last bastion of defense. They observe him intently, trying to determine if his words are indications of an unhinged mind or simple hyperbole. He notes how their numbers have dwindled of late, some of his brightest students lured away by rivals. The ones who remain doubt their decision to stay, checking him surreptitiously for signs of senility.

His foray into hypnosis has proven to be divisive, controversial. The medical community splintered to the point of schism. Regularly, his lectures devolve into discord—factions in the audience shouting each other down. The war waged in public and in print. Each defection compounding the sense that he is under siege.

In the annex at night, he spreads pictures of Augustine across the floor until her body reforms before him. Thighs, sex, breasts, each segmented from the other, discreetly boxed and framed. A geometry of squares flattened under some great weight. He gazes down at the mosaic he has created. The chimera of her body merged with the photographic beast. Deformed, plated, gargantuan. The figure of a giantess, growing out of control.

As swiftly as he assembles it, he destroys it, pulling each appendage in opposite directions until she is drawn and quartered. Her body wracked, twisted. Limbs askew.

∞

He tries to remember life before the asylum, but his only memories are of Augustine. He is the father of a thousand children, all of them bearing her face—each image an embryo filling his belly. His body riddled with them. Recollections that will never fade or dim, that will never diminish. Endlessly reproducing, crowding out his other organs. His heart contracted against the pressure.

Memory is the seed of personality, he tells the audience. It determines who and what we are—the legacy we leave behind. Alter Augustine's memories and she will lose every notion of her identity. Erase an image, and you erase her past, annihilate her future. It is easy enough to accomplish. After all, what is memory but a pregnancy of images? And with hypnosis, we can implant and abort them at will.

He thinks of M, catches her eye, and knows she is thinking the same. Wondering whether it is a threat he could in fact fulfill.

∞

At times, you seem determined to hasten my demise, invoking seizure after seizure as if hoping my body will dismember itself in the fierceness of the attack. At other times, you throw yourself at my mercy, lay your life in my hands.

Even if I instruct her to, you tell the audience, Augustine will not strangle me, and thus we can observe the limits of hypnotic commands—she may squeeze but she will not crush.

And I place my hands around your neck, feel the varicose veins and knotty carotid, your skin that has already assumed the velvety softness of approaching decay, feel the air rasping through your windpipe, the way the blood grows sluggish if I tighten my grip. How often have you commanded me to obey, to react without question? If I did so now, it would be the end of you, *Maître*, of all of this, of me, perhaps. The audience a many-eyed witness, certain to convict.

What would the world be without you, *Maître*? How would it go on? Effortlessly, perhaps, or lamentingly, listing on its axis.

Inquisition

You bring me a letter telling me M is dead. Delivered in the middle of the night, in darkness. You do not wait to hear its contents. They spill like entrails on the floor around me. The ink on the paper still damp, staining my fingers—my white nightgown smeared with black spots, spores that germinate and scatter, spread head to toe like mold. The cloth a skin that I shed in my room, putrid and decayed, the flesh beneath already festering, infected by the news. *Maître, mon dieu,* M is dead, and I am alone. I dig my nails deep into my forearms, raking downward, the blood and ink mixing. No one comes to comfort me. No one cares what damage is done. My nightgown in shreds on the floor; it is all they find of me when they check again, hours later. The window shattered, the mark of a body landing on the ground below. I am up and running in an instant, the bottom of my feet covered with clumps of mud, a low stone wall claiming skin as I slide down it, leaving an indistinct outline on granite, an afterimage on a negative plate. The cemetery lies within the hospital's grounds, surrounded by the hunched bodies of weeping willows. Flashbulbs are strung from the trees. Epistles hang from the branches, each proclaiming that M is dead. Hands dangling beside them, rife with gnarled veins and lifelines ended abruptly. The odor of wet woolen leaves blankets everything. Leaflets and letters penned in your hand litter the mourner's path. In the blackness, headstones rear out of the ground as white as any page. M is dead. The words are carved deep in the marble or emerge suddenly on the surface of stone as if steeped in developer. Beheaded statues point the way to the only unmarked grave, like perverse weather vanes heralding me on. M is dead, *Maître*, and I am naked on my knees in the dirt, digging. I make my mouth a shovel, gouging and spitting out soil, my palms are buckets, my nails rakes. I am weeding you out, M, resurrecting you from seed, the eggs of blowflies beading my tonsils, my throat a larval cave. The maggots burrow deep into my lungs like seeds aspirated. I swallow them, afraid they will find you before I do, infest your body and rot it out before I can reach it, before I can know with certainty that you lie here. M is dead, *Monsieur?* It seems impossible. Are you dead, M? That cannot be what the letter said, that you are buried in a box, sealed in darkness. That vines sprout from between your ribs, your skin spotted with poisonous mushrooms that breed inside your body, erupting from the pores. When I find you, M, I will gorge myself, ingest the soft lobes, and acquire the breath of toxins and spores. I will become parasitic, clinging to your skin, feeding off your decay. Growing ripe and beautiful. I will burn any tongue that touches me, scar any fingers that dare to feel my fungal gills, the crenellated fringe bearding my chin. I will turn brown to match you, turn blue, green, yellow. I will be a death cap, a destroying angel, virulent and hidden behind my partial veil. I will keep everyone away from us, M—my mushroom *mûrissant, musquée*, my amanita muscaria, warted and scarred. How is it that you are dead? How is it that I cannot exhume any part of you? That even as I lie here, the rigor settles into my limbs so that I cannot bury myself in earth and leaf mold. I cannot stop from being seen. Spotted by the interns in a matter of hours, the only living thing in this rotting ground, the only corpse risen to the surface. They will take me, M, but they will not weave a metaphor fine enough to shroud you in.

∽

My grief will not abate, *Maître*. It is boundless, immeasurable. It is pure negation.

You ply me with soporifics, sedatives, giving me bromides and laudanum daily. And I live in a perpetual daze, lightheaded, faint, unable to walk a straight line, unable to think. My body convulsing up to twenty times an hour, my face contorted by stabbing pains for which the interns give me morphine, injected straight under the skin.

In the amphitheatre, you hold up a syringe filled with a cloudy liquid, explain that it is a concoction you have created that can transmute flesh into other substances. The assistants overpowering me when I struggle, allowing you to inject the fluid into my wrist. You tell me it will turn me to wax, and I watch, shocked, as the liquid enters the vein, turning the skin dull and lusterless as it moves through my body, coagulating tissue into tallow. You light a flame, hold it in your cupped hands, bring it close to my skin and then move it farther away. The heat singes the hairs on my arms, and the flesh begins to puddle and pool, dripping onto the floor in fatty globs that harden on the wood. The pain is unbearable as you melt body parts without hesitation, the assistants restraining me as I bend desperately to scoop the wax before it hardens, trying to reform an arm, a breast, a leg. You look only at the audience, unmoved by my screams, as I watch my skin bubble and burst. I am an effigy burned to the marrow, Icarus plunging to the ground.

Hypnosis allows us to transform the very materiality of the body with a mere suggestion, you say. If we tell Augustine she is made of glass, she will not move an inch without taking infinite precautions. The slightest tap is enough to convince her that an appendage is irreparably shattered, and she subsequently will not respond to any provocation of that limb, even pain. She will remember where each shard has supposedly fallen and avoid them assiduously. If one forces her to walk across the area, she will react as if she has sliced her foot, and a glance at the skin will reveal contusions, the blood vessels ruptured as if the sole has suffered a multitude of wounds.

Such suggestions seem ludicrous to us, but we must remember that the hysteric experiences life like the memory of a story. We can insert ourselves into her fantasies, change their course and consistency, like novelists rewriting a plot. We only need apply a little ingenuity to elicit the scenario of our choosing, to set our drama in motion.

Sometimes we supplement a simple verbal suggestion with a more tangible artifact—a letter, for example—making the lie that much more authoritative in her eyes.

Only then do I realize the lengths you will go to, the crimes you have willingly committed—pen in hand, an envelope delivered. The field of my vision bathed in red. It colors your mouth, your hands, the center of your pupils. Your fingers staining me like a murderer's, leaving prints all over my body.

I curse at you, call you beast, brute, spitting until my throat goes dry, until my lips crack and bleed. Tongue cleaved to the roof of my mouth as if you have called a holy wrath down upon me. *Salaud. Bête. Diable.* My heart racing until you restrain me. *La camisole de force* wrapping around me like a body embracing, bracing me, begging me to be still.

Something has broken between us. The vestiges of an unspoken, intangible truce. Ours was never a benign fascination, but a canker. Now, it erupts into malignancy, an infection that forms an abscess between us. Caustic. Blistering. That which touches it corrodes.

I employ movements meant as insults, insurrections, revolts—thrashing violently, foregrounding the body's baseness rather than its beauty. I move suddenly, despairingly, breach and then break our contract, demeaning us both in the process. You refuse to photograph these fits, try to erase their existence, until I loose them upon the audience, gesticulating my odium and exultation. The fury in your eyes, then, beautiful to behold.

In the amphitheatre, I accuse you of murder, level charges at the crowd, my memories returning in flames, raging throughout the building.

For a time, I see only in red, a color your photographs cannot reproduce. I dream of bloodlettings and slaughterhouses, carcasses exsanguinated and hung from hooks, and everywhere the odor of iron. Animals roam the killing floor, skinned and staggering, aortas exposed, wearing bridles of crushed capillaries, their teeth clamped around bits made of bone. And I awaken in a bed of menstrual blood, blanketed in it.

I refuse to reveal these visions, *Monsieur*. I reach into my mouth as though I would dislodge my tongue at its base. I have already given you too much that I do not have, and it has all turned to hatred, to shame.

Under the power of intoxication, you resurrect M at will. Enact in-numerable executions. Until I can barely gauge the reality of any given instant. Never knowing when to expect these encounters, whether to welcome or despise them. Each one its own type of inebriation.

I cannot think or clear my head of you, M, *mon amour, mon aimant,* my beloved addiction. You enter my veins, course through my bloodstream, leaving me dispossessed. A heady substance, capable of buckling limbs. Without you, I pine and clamor, cramp and palpitate, suffer the most exquisite withdrawal. It is an agonizing abstinence—a descent from which there is no return.

Mon cher, I cannot, will not, tolerate your absence.

I cry out for more drugs, steal them from the infirmary, several times indulging to the point of overdose. M in my arms again, pressing tongue to tongue, breast to breast, until I cannot tell if the shudder-ing inside me is greater than that without. *M, je t'aime,* I whisper, *M, je t'aime.*

We rehearse in a secret theatre, a stage sequestered in the Bois de Boulogne, at the end of a long, untrammeled path. We are actors in a drama of revolution, standing abreast in solidarity. We mime victory, resist defeat, all to an audience of trees, newts, and grubs. We turn over clods of earth, inviting the spiders and centipedes to watch us practice our lines. Silkworms weaving our costumes thread by thread. Earthworms evacuating soil from their bodies to create a softer stage. After we are finished performing, we lie in beds of grass and lichen, our bodies pollen-dusted, brushed in gold.

You exhibit my reunions with M in the amphitheatre, invoking them before the camera like any common purveyor of smut. Until even they are ruined. My desire deadened the instant you detect it, so that

time after time, you capture not the moment of pleasure, but its absence. A Peeping Tom arriving once the spectacle has ended. Even the
photographs fail to arouse, the nudity sexless and sterile, a frank ac-
knowledgment of desire's defeat. The negatives unfit to print, wasted.

My only gratification: your inability to demand resolution, to
obtain release.

∞

Days spent in semi-trance. Hardly ever rising from the bed. We are
trapped in narratives of your invention, cast in tragedies. M stabbed.
Decapitated. Shot in the head in the Bois de Boulogne, the scene
rendered in black and white, inky blood pouring from the wound,
grey matter spattered on my hands, white slivers of bone.

And the black blush of M's lips is like a dog's. Rubbery, livid,
salivating. Around us, the forest is consumed by flames, pale tongues
devouring the black bodies of the trees. The curtain falling to the
stage, pooling darkly amidst the blacker blood. A fount gushing from
my nose, sanguine and unceasing.

During the height of delirium, M appears to me disguised as the
Comtesse de la Motte—wearing her collar of diamonds and broken vertebrae, still dressed in the masculine garb that enabled her
escape. Her jawline fringed by fractures. We stand at a window inside
a countryside estate, and for a moment, I experience a sensation of
freedom, an existence far beyond the asylum walls. But it is not long
before the carriage comes, driven by dead men, pulled by beasts the
size of dogs with long flat black ears, crows hovering above. The men
are coming to bring us back, it is certain, as is our refusal. I take M's
hand in mine as we step to the window ledge and then into air.

This is the power that remains to me. The power of finale.

ᘡ

In the amphitheatre, as I watch, the boards of the stage buckle and twist, spring upright, burgeoning branches that divide and entwine, until I find myself in a forest of elm and maple, fir and pine. In the clearing, a group of men gathers, bending boughs and bracken, creating a cage in the shape of a body. They are building a wicker man. Enormous. Archaic. Poor men perform the labor, steady workers unconcerned with what they have been asked to do.

From the underbrush, they drag the victim, and I realize that it is you, M, your body bruised from struggling against them, your ankles shackled. The men treat you roughly, heave you inside the giant's body. You struggle, like a heart beating amidst the empty chest, the wooden ribs so close together that escape is impossible.

There is nothing I can do to stop them—bound to a chair, clamped by restraints. They will burn you. Sacrifice you to this simulacrum.

Our doubles always come back to haunt us—the forests alight with flames, the darkrooms illuminated by flashes of phosphorous. Recreating us *ad infinitum*. How many executions must we endure, *mon cher,* before we put a stop to this? They will use you against me, endlessly, ever ingenious in the arts of delay, distraction, suffering. I realize now—there is no rescue for the doomed, only repetition, failure. Forgive me. This final time. There will be no more resurrections. I must let you die, let them take your beautiful body and expose it to fire. The flames licking until your skin adheres to its many tongues. Your body raw. Now truly naked.

I breathe your ashes into me. M, my martyr. They sacrifice us both to angry gods. We are birds entranced and trapped, feathers set ablaze. I will rise as a reckoning, a winged fury, I promise you.

ᘡ

You hate my screams, so I shriek for hours. My mouth a macula at the center of your lens. Foregrounded. Distinct.

You rave that it ruins your photos—the black hole like a defect in the frame, invasive, inhuman, requiring drastic retouching with paintbrushes and pens. The orifice a fissure disturbing your focus. And the more you gaze at it, *Maître*, the more you long to crawl inside.

The patient's screams are ugly, brutal things, you say, devolving into barks, howls, caterwauls, croaks. The hysteric becomes an animal, she grunts and groans, but her cries are meaningless. They are mere imitations of sound, the mark of imagination exasperated, speech annihilated. An inverse swallowing. Her mouth opened wide, she gasps as if suffocated, curls into herself and then expels this guttural, deafening clamor. Recalling the old description of the nightmare as "the dream which eats the dream."

The pitch of my scream leaves vials of smelling salts shattered, audience members clutching at their ears. I stick my tongue out and bite it, spitting blood on the pillows, rolling my eyes to white. My hand, in apparent seizure, striking out to land stingingly across your face.

This is *clownisme*, you declare, the final and most useless phase of the attack, during which the patient shouts insults, grows insolent, begs to leave. Instead of the classic *attitudes passionelles*, the patient delivers violent, illogical movements. Even her nudity is revolting.

Watching her, we are filled with a horrible emptiness, an antipathy, as if we are witnessing the abject nature of the body, the brutality that triumphs at the moment of death, when the muscles lose control, bladder and bowels soiling the bedclothes.

Your voice is riddled with malice. Spittle expelled from the corners of your mouth into my own. It is you who tastes of decay. Your mouth a cavity disseminating plagues. The audience leaning so close they feed off your breath, eye me with disgust, turn away, turn only towards you.

For this, I have given my body. Muscles ragged with tears, skeleton marred by unnecessary breakages, veins depleted. For this, *Maître,* for you.

I remember years when I could not tell you from me, when you sat inside me as surely as my bones, wearing me from the inside out. I was the skin covering your muscles, lungs, heart. There was no part of me not filled by you. Infiltrated as a body is by disease.

I claw at my chest. I cry out convulsing, and like a mirror of my every movement, you raise your chilled fingers for a moment to your heart, feeling a beating that is closer to bursting. Something in your eyes showing through for a moment—the look of a man caught amidst too many reflections, terrified that he will be forced to look into the face of his death. But for you, there is something more than this. A fear that your legacy will be destroyed.

Now that every fantasy has failed us, *Maître,* we must admit defeat. Let us play our finale and be done. Let us draw our weapons and duel to the death.

Augustine, you say, and I begin to scream again. Timeless, unending screams, screams that suck your breath into mine, absorb it, as if a magnet has been placed in the back of my throat. Leaving you gasping, mouth agape, cheeks gaunt. Breathless.

Your eyes settle on me, and you recognize your succubus, your death incarnate, your Augustine. Disfigured. Horrible. As you created me.

I rise from the table, stand on the edge of the stage, face you, face the interns, the audience, and bow.

Messieurs, mesdames, I declare, I am cured. And I walk offstage, not waiting long enough to watch the denouement—jaws dropping like curtains behind me.

$$\backsim$$

He refuses the ending she has offered him, drags her back to the amphitheatre, ignoring her disavowal of the disease. Their demonstrations transformed into battles, acts of attrition.

In the evenings, he returns to the annex—the room covered with her portraits. Augustine lying, sleeping, seizing, posing with her arm raised like a student in a classroom. *Maître. Mon professeur.* The more he looks at it, the more it seems to him a challenge of all that he is—this one gesture making everything irrelevant. The audience's approval, their amazement, negated.

Even when she is lying before him, he envisions her in the back of the amphitheatre. Always seated at a different desk, as if she has somehow sent her spirit out. And he is haunted by this image—her arm raised in a defense that is also a defiance. A question that he cannot answer. A pupil he cannot appease.

He calls on her repeatedly—yes, Augustine, yes? But she never responds, performing instead this maddening mime.

He tells the audience, Augustine has become unmanageable, as she strikes him for the second time in the middle of the lecture. He says, Augustine has become uncooperative. Everything she does is extravagant: leaping out of windows, climbing trees, scaling the roof of the asylum naked. After minor vexations, she shatters windows, reduces furniture to splinters, roams the courtyard barefoot, speaking endlessly of escape. And we grow tired of her outbursts. Tired—perhaps—of everything.

Watching from the wings, she rubs one index finger over the other, in chastisement, as if she is scolding him or throwing a spark to cast the whole room alight.

Fugue

ON THE DAY OF SAINT-MARTIN, your saint's day, the entire asylum prepares for the *fête*. The interns having planned pantomimes to honor you, skits they have been practicing for weeks, reciting the lines in the hallways to an audience of madwomen. Today, the asylum is full of Charcots, imitators in monocles and hats, interns who have powdered their hair with talc to match your grey or darkened their eyes with coal dust to mimic your sunken sockets. One cannot move more than a few feet without running into a *maître*. One young man holds a key under his tongue, pockets filled with francs, breasts bound to flatness. He has a masculine walk, somewhat swaggering, and greets his colleagues with prompt dismissiveness, eager to be on his way.

The merriment in the air is already tinged with subtle mockery, a portent of what is to come. You have convinced yourself that they hold you in such reverence, *Maître*, such high regard—your pupils, looking through the lens you have provided, seeing everything just as you do. But once you have died, they will ruin you, your reputation. They will write about the imprudence of old age, your slight failures, your worst audacities. Even those who defend you will call you naïve, too easily swayed, too prone to flights of fancy. Your diligent students, your disciples, how they will turn on you. You will become the hysterical Charcot, the doddering professor hoodwinked by your own hypnotic arts.

I can see it in them already—this desire to undo you. To outdo you. To tear you apart. You are Actaeon and they are your hounds. You will die in their jaws, punished by the gods for looking at me. For looking too long, not looking away.

Today, you do not even notice me, dressed as I am in trousers, hat, my hair tucked up underneath. I am just another masquerade-*maître,* your likeness, tipping his hat to you and walking out the front door.

Outside, the pathways spread like synapses, leading away from the pulse and throb of the asylum's center, away from you.

Women stand scattered amidst the open colonnades, their bodies forming the crippled pillars of the institution. Frozen in contorted positions, they voice no alarm. Only their eyes follow my flight. *Les folles de la Sâlpetrière, les hystériques de Charcot.* On the day of your death, we will dream of you, *Maître,* dream the darkness into your eyes, the final rupture of aorta and ventricles, the blown pupils. We, who dreamed you into existence, will dream you out again. *Cher Maître.* It didn't need to be this way. I would have cradled your head in my lap, placed cool fingers on your temples, stroked the veins through their spasms, taught you to weather the stillness with patience and grace. I would have stayed for the duration of my life, watching your fingers articulate the air. Devoted. Instead, I will dream your death, wherever I may be, and you will dream of me, far from here, my boot pressed against your neck until the pulsing stops.

I stride purposefully, each step seeming to carry me back in time, to an earlier era. Leaving behind the hum of the Division Parîset, I enter the old-world misery of the Cour Sainte-Claire. A light rain is falling, and the edifices ooze a jaundiced, liver yellow. The air exuding the subtle fragrance of troubled sleep—moist, intimate, with the slight acridity of sweat. On one side looms the Batimênt de la Force, the ancient prison. Behind its walls the incurables wait—wards of women committed for life. On the other side, the buildings hold *les reposantes, les grandes infirmes.* This is the quarter of lodgings. Those housed here do not expect to leave. They wait only for the box. To be interred in the adjacent cemetery, or to be carved neck to navel—parts preserved in formaldehyde or reproduced in plaster and placed on a museum shelf.

You will never claim my body now. Only the doubles remain—those I could not destroy, plates doused in developer, sculptures smashed. I wonder what you will do when you discover them, what fate would befall me if I were to be caught. And I recall the Comtesse de la Motte, terrorized by memories, mistakenly believing they had tracked her down, hurling herself from the ramparts to avoid such a return. Will I too experience such dread, hear in every footstep the sound of pursuit?

You spoke to me once of a hunt you had witnessed. You said, Augustine, can you imagine, they take a pack of dogs—and you shuddered, *Maître,* at the thought of this—and they let them chew the fox to shreds, the hunter on his horse never risking the slightest harm. And you said, barbaric. You said, brutal. Your mouth curled in contempt and disgust. As if for a brief and fleeting moment, you could feel what it was like to be this hunted hounded thing.

You would never show me such mercy.

I quicken my pace, walk as fast as I can without drawing attention—having plotted my route so many nights on a map unfolded in my lap, my finger following circuitous passages, insular enclosures, quarters without exit.

I pass the graveyard where I once believed M to be buried. I do not even pause to pay my respects—knowing M is not bound by earth or root, but carried within me, as vital as plasma and lymph.

The cemetery wall marks a boundary beyond which I've never ventured. I proceed without a backward glance, past the margins. The grounds stretch on indefinitely—courtyard upon courtyard, like a string of reflections. As if the space is expanding to keep me contained.

In the late afternoon, the air fills with the scent of gunpowder, saltpeter, and the buildings turn the fitful violet of a body deprived of breath, shifting arthritically in the oncoming chill of evening. The chimneys and spires give the edifices a guarded appearance, as if a bird landing on the rooftop would be skewered by some sharpened, unseen spike. The buildings bristle at my back. And I realize then how exposed I am, the windows dark-lidded, opaque, the grounds empty of any body except my own.

Moving through the squared entryway of the Cour de Mazarin, I pass at last beyond the compound's inner sanctum. The trees reach out crippled hands to catch me, their shadows stretched by the low angle of the sun as it sets.

The asylum's outer walls tower above everything. They emit a magnetic draw, evoking the iron-grey of lodestone, of hematite. Their surface smooth and impenetrable from this distance. As I draw closer, the walls grow taller, reaching unreasonable heights, the granite leaching color out of the surroundings, suffusing everything with the deadened hue of stone. I trail the colossal expanse until I become winded, my chest constricted as if the walls have tumbled down on top of me, cracking ribs, collapsing lungs.

The archway appears unexpectedly—the opening revealed only by a deeper darkness, as if all light is extinguished by the thirsty slabs of slate. The chained gate glinting like fangs within. I push the key into the lock, hands shaking. It seems unimaginable that outside this courtyard lies Paris. For years, I have lived in a different city, miles and decades distant—an interior city, full of wonders, full of terrors.

He sits in the hospital's makeshift museum—a narrow, cluttered room divided lengthwise by a red-and-gold-striped carpet. Lamps are spread at intervals to spotlight an array of scopes, meters, and electrical equipment. The countertops and cabinets crowded by a profusion of jars in which viscous liquids surround unidentifiable organs. In some spots liquid has leaked from the containers, leaching into the walls, leaving ulcers that lacerate wood. The display as garish and threadbare as any hall of oddities.

Everywhere he turns, there is a person who is not a person. A casting or a copper bust. A flat, discolored drawing. Skeletons hang in tall glass cabinets, skulls tilted sideways to rest on scapulae as if even the bones are exhausted. He cradles his head in his hands, wonders if she will ever find her way back to him, present him once again with her body—the future corpse that he cared for, ministered to, cultivated. A promise forever deferred, a consummation denied.

Obsessing over the hours wasted on self-restraint and what they have cost him, he closes his eyes, reimagines their sessions together. Her body spread out before him as he indulges the lethal impulses of the overcurious child, who breaks open his plaything, destroys it, pursues at all costs his desire to know.

Coda
1893

IN THE *ATELIER D'AUTOPSIE,* his flesh grows pale and waxen, skin mottled as the blood begins to coagulate and cool, lips and gums already retracting. His face reshapes itself by the minute, discovering pleats and hollows, new ways to drape tissue over bone, as the cells release toxins, shrivel, and collapse inward. Someone applies a putty to the skin, followed by a coating of plaster, a substance so often shaped by his hands, administered now like a bandage for a wound treated far too late.

A death mask, that is what they are making. Despite his retreat inward, he feels it, knows it to be final. The replica will not even resemble him, he thinks. His features already altered by the chemistry of decay. They have applied the mixture too late. Everything, in fact, is too late now. The cool sweep of her fingers across his brow, his cheekbones, as she smooths out the clots and bulges in the plaster before it sets, her caresses coming only after his skin has been covered.

She places magnets on his body to draw the coldness out, restoring mobility to his rigored muscles, taking needles from her arms to stitch closed the arterial tears. She shocks his heart back to beating, his limbs to moving, his voice to asking her, Augustine, seize for me, Augustine, come.

The feeling is strong enough to wake him, to make him gasp—this understanding of what he has lost.

When the time comes, there will be no final epiphany, no Augustine. She is miles away. There will be only a cloying slop and interns molding a mask of a man with a quickly fading resemblance to himself, *Monsieur Charcot, le Maître de la Salpêtrière, professeur de rien.*

He continues to lie in darkness, waits for her to appear before him as she has every night since her escape. Watching like a man entranced as she ties her hair in ribbons, wraps herself in veils.

He tells her, Augustine, your seizures are like stories, continually unfolding. And he opens her page by page. Reading the text as though he himself has written it. Admiring the way the weathered spine bends under his fingers.

She opens her mouth, puts her hand inside, as if to draw something out. And says, the words are tourniquets, *Monsieur.* They do not heal. They signify nothing. Only something stopped.

Afterword

A Note on the Sourcing, Research, and Writing of *Asylum*

THIS NOVEL OWES A MAJOR DEBT to Georges Didi-Huberman's *Invention de l'hystérie: Charcot et l'iconographie photographique de la Salpêtrière* (Macula, 1982), which served as the primary inspiration for much of the material and metaphorical structure of the book. I first stumbled upon the history of Charcot and Augustine and a reference to Didi-Huberman's work while reading Elaine Showalter's *The Female Malady* (Penguin, 1985) as an undergraduate at Brown University. At the time, there was no English translation of Didi-Huberman's book available, so I ordered the French edition and set about translating it with my rusty French skills. The book is extremely complex, with rich and evocative writing, circuitous sentences, challenging theory, striking illustrations, and an innovative organizational structure of its own (due largely in part, no doubt, to Didi-Huberman's background as an art historian).

I considered trying to publish the translation. However, it turned out that during the many years I had spent working on *Asylum*, someone else had already done so. I didn't become aware until several years after the fact. At that point, I read and reread Alisa Hartz's scholarly work (MIT Press 2003). Ultimately, *Asylum* draws upon my own translation of Didi-Huberman's text, as well as Hartz's book. There were important differences between our translations (though mine might have been born out of error), including our translation of one of Augustine's quotes (a slightly altered version of which appears in the final paragraph of *Asylum)*.

Like the "protean" disease of hysteria, in which patients were known to usurp and appropriate the gestures, words, and identities of others, my novel absorbs and contains ideas, quotations, section titles, and metaphors from the source material I used. There are no individual notations to mark those references, but anyone who reads Didi-Huberman's book will see the places in which I allowed his creation to bleed into my own. I felt it was necessary to blend voices and ideas without distracting the reader with citations and quotation marks. I have included actual words spoken by Augustine, Charcot, and others in these pages. Some appear untouched, some are intermingled with my own writing.

I tried to remain faithful to the real methodologies and treatments practiced at the Salpêtrière and the basic veracity of events, including the incredible ending that Augustine orchestrated for herself. There are many historically accurate incidents and experiments recreated in these pages. Augustine did have an imaginary lover, named M, who appeared during her fits. She did break out of the asylum one evening and try to dig up M's grave after receiving a falsified letter that M had died. In the real history, M was male; however, I wanted to create M as a genderless figure whose fluid identity could overlap with many characters and concepts within the novel.

In several key matters, I did not approach this project in a strictly historical sense. Above all, I wanted to avoid assigning a cause or pronouncing a psychological verdict on Augustine and hysteria itself. I wanted to immerse the reader (and myself) in the midst of the bizarre, seductive, and disturbing relationship between Augustine, Charcot, and the asylum. Rather than searching for causation—the relentless pursuit of so many physicians and psychiatrists who wanted an "answer" and "cure" for female madness—I chose to approach the relationship between Augustine and Charcot on its own terms, with the asylum as their sole shared context. In doing so, I hope to avoid reducing Augustine to a "case study." I was not interested in grounding the seemingly inexplicable phenomena of hysteria in biographical reality. I wanted to see what would happen if I amplified that unreality—if I entered it. Freud believed that returning patients to wellness involved filling in the gaps and fixing the fragmentation within their narrative life "stories." I set out to write a hysterical narrative, to embrace fragmentation, to create holes, and to see what happens when we stare into the abyss and the abyss stares back at us (to paraphrase Nietzsche).

Some of the symptoms and experiences attributed to Augustine in fact occurred to other patients at the asylum. I omitted the other doctors and photographers who were part of the "production" of hysteria at the Salpêtrière (and, in some places, I have attributed their words to Charcot), in order to create a claustrophobic focus on doctor and patient.

I do not imagine "my" Augustine as the teenager that she really was. I do not attribute to my Augustine the biographical facts of the real Augustine's life. I found, during my examination of primary sources online, which became available later in the course of my work, that even Didi-Huberman took Augustine's quotations and words sometimes very much out of context. It seems that Augustine inspires invention; she is simultaneously an overeager and unwilling muse to everyone who encounters her and views the photographs of her, including the Surrealists, who used her posthumously as a "mascot."

A very long time has passed since I started work on this novel—the first seeds of the book emerged as far back as 1998. For years, I struggled to assemble hundreds of fragments into an order that remained true to my metaphorical homage to Didi-Huberman's work and that also held together as a novel. There were periods of months and maybe even years when I avoided working on the project and felt like a failed writer. At times, I thought I would never finish the book. Thankfully, that didn't turn out to be the case. The acknowledgments pay tribute to the indispensable helpers I had along the way.

Written January 15, 2018

Acknowledgments

THIS NOVEL WOULD NOT EXIST without the support and dedication of the following people, to whom I owe a debt of thanks: To Michelle Dotter and Dzanc Books for fulfilling my keenest hopes by accepting the novel and its vision wholeheartedly. To Lance Olsen, Tina May Hall, and Jessie van Eerden for championing the book into existence. To Ted Pelton, *Plinth, Sidebrow,* and *Fourteen Hills* for publishing excerpts and early versions of *Asylum.*

To Margaret Klawuun for introducing me to Elaine Showalter's work and, by extension, to Augustine. To Carole Maso for reading the earliest incarnation of the novel. To the Millay Colony for the Arts for time and space—as far back as 2000, I was taping up photographs of Augustine in my studio in Edna St. Vincent Millay's barn. To Lynne Tirrell and Tim Sperry for providing me with a makeshift "writer's retreat" in their home when the book was still thousands of disjointed paragraphs spread across their dining room table.

To Susan Edmunds for her brilliant and exhaustive attention to the manuscript in its troublesome middle years. To my professors, fellow graduate students, and fellow writers for their advice, edits, and attentiveness: Brian Evenson, George Saunders, Mary Caponegro, Rahul Mehta, Phil LaMarche, and Stephanie Carpenter. Special thanks to Erin Brooks Worley and Christian TeBordo for inspiring me to persevere when my confidence was at its lowest. To Laird Hunt, Shay Youngblood, Susan Berkley, Jane Davis, Nicole Pollentier, and Farooq Ahmed for reading the near-final manuscript and pushing me to believe in my vision of what the novel could be.

To Arthur Flowers, whom I can never thank enough, for his persistent encouragement over many years, his willingness to spend precious time reading the piece when it was just a jumble of fragments, and for giving the project the nickname "The Hissies," which somehow made it so much more enjoyable and manageable throughout the years to come. To my friend Stephanie Krause for fantastic moments of levity and for careful and caring edits.

To my mother, Judy Shope, for instilling in me an early love of myth and literature. To my father, Robert Shope, for immersing me in symbolism and analytical thought. To my grandparents, Mildred and Arthur Eisenstein, whom I miss to this day. To Nancy, Kenny, and Michael Eisenstein for their love and enthusiasm. To my husband, Chris Narozny, for being a role model of dedication to one's craft and for reminding me that writing is a core piece of my identity, even when I fiercely long to avoid it. I am lucky to share the writer's path with you.

And finally, as always, to my sister, Nikki Dublin Shepherd, for having my back from start to finish, for helping me shape the chaos, for parsing and scrutinizing every word (often repeatedly), and for giving me the faith, confidence, and ability to endure. You will always be my most cherished editor and reader. You immersed yourself in this novel so deeply that I swear you absorbed it into your tissue. You are my *semblable*, my second Augustine, and my soul.

About the Author

Nina Shope is the author of *Hangings: Three Novellas*, published by Starcherone Books. *Asylum* is her first full-length novel. Her fiction has appeared in *Quarter After Eight, Fourteen Hills, 3rd Bed, Open City, Sleeping Fish, Salt Hill,* and elsewhere. Her stories have been anthologized in *PP/FF: An Anthology, New Standards: The First Decade of Fiction at Fourteen Hills,* and *Wreckage of Reason: XXperimental Women Writers Writing in the 21st Century.* She holds a BA from Brown University and an MFA from Syracuse University. She currently lives in Denver, Colorado, with her husband, author Christopher Narozny, and their corgi.